I0726741

SECRETS, LOVERS AND LIES

The German Conspiracy in America

NATASHA

WORKBOOK PRESS LLC
187 E Warm Springs Rd,
Suite B285, Las Vegas, NV 89119, USA

Website: https://workbookpress.com/
Hotline: 1-888-818-4856
Email: admin@workbookpress.com

Ordering Information:
Quantity sales. Special discounts are available on quantity purchases by corporations, associations, and others.
For details, contact the publisher at the address above.

ISBN-13:   978-1-953839-48-0 (Paperback Version)
                978-1-953839-47-3 (Digital Version)

REV. DATE: 10/12/2022

Secrets, Lovers & Lies

By Natasha

CONTENTS

ONE

Walking Away

It was 1977, the year I gave up the priesthood. Had I known the truth I would never have questioned my leaving. It was the place to hide from the world. Had I known the truth I would never have wanted to live. It was a union with Satan, and it lived with our family under the guise of love.

Today I walked away from my parish, smiled and inhaled the fresh, warm air. I was twenty-nine, a strong, six-foot male with the natural healthy desire to love a woman and tired of hiding it. I am thankful for the education I received but now I am in the direction I once ignored. It is over. I am free to be a man.

I thought back to when I had first entered Saint Joseph's Seminary, to the day I was ordained. My family was very happy, especially my mother who was very active in our church and introduced me to what it offered. Had I known the truth about our need to be connected to the church my life would have been different.

Shortly after leaving the Jesuit order, a seminarian friend called about a position that was open teaching Ancient History in Boston, Mass. The Superintendent of Schools was very anxious to hire me but later I became apprehensive about what awaited me at this racially mixed, problematic, C. P. Rowley Junior High.

The rest of the summer flew by and the day finally arrived when I entered the hallway of the Rowley School for my first teacher's meeting. The outline of a female figure standing alone down the corridor caught my attention. My eyes moved over the generous curves of her body and as I walked closer to her, our eyes met. What a beautiful face, I thought to myself as I said, "Sorry if I've been staring at you, but with your red hair and blue eyes you look like one of those beautiful Irish girls I saw last summer when I visited Ireland."

"I'm sorry to disappoint you," she said as she smiled, "but I've never been to Ireland and I'm not Irish, I'm Jewish. My name is Judith Loeb."

"My name's Michael, Michael Ulrike, and I guess you can tell from my name that I'm not Irish either." She laughed, "You're right about that." And a beautiful dimple appeared on her left cheek.

"Have you traveled to many countries besides Ireland?" she asked.

"Yes, whenever I had a vacation. Last year I went to Germany to visit relatives." I answered.

"I had relatives in Germany, also," she said, "but the only ones that are left are the few that survived the concentration camps."

"My family is lucky to be alive." I told her. "They were among the first Christians that joined the Resistance to the Nazis."

As we talked, I found myself very much at ease in the company of Judith, who was also starting her first teaching position.

"Have you always lived in New York?" I asked.

"I lived there all my life. I went to Hunter College there, majored in art and then I went to the New York School of Art and Design."

"How do you feel being away from home?"

"I wasn't too happy leaving my family and friends but since teaching jobs are so hard to come by I feel lucky to have gotten one at all. This is my first chance to be really on my own and I think I'm going to enjoy it, after I make some friends. I don't know anyone here yet. Are you from Boston?" she inquired.

"No, I've only been here since last month. I grew up in New Jersey and

Maryland." I looked at the big school clock In front of us. "It's getting late. Let's go to the cafeterior for the teachers' meeting, Judith."

"That is a good idea but please call me Jody, instead of Judith, all my friends do."

When we entered the cafeterior Theodore Bradshaw, the principal, better known as Ted, was getting ready to speak. He was a tall, large-framed man in his early sixties with steel grey eyes. He opened the meeting in a loud friendly voice.

"Good morning, teachers. Well, summer has come and gone and here we are again, ready for another good year together. Today we welcome two new teachers to our fold who come highly recommended. Those of us who appreciate feminine pulchritude have certainly noticed the beautiful red head who is going to be our new art teacher. Judith Loeb, will you please stand?" I watched Jody as she slowly rose and everyone applauded. Principal

Bradshaw cleared his throat.

"And, for the women in our school we hired that good-looking, tall blonde man sitting in the rear, to teach ancient history. Michael Ulrike, would you please stand?"

Amused at his introduction, I stood up, received my share of applause and quickly sat down.

Mr. Bradshaw smilingly went on. "The first thing I want to say is if any problems arise in this school please continue to bring them to me before you do anything. I will help in any situation I can. Just keep in mind we are all one big happy family here at the Rowley and we intend to keep it this way! Now let's all enjoy ourselves with some cake and coffee."

Within the next few minutes I saw that the teachers were very friendly with each other and both Jody and I were made to feel welcome. Tony DeAngelio, the math teacher, and Alan Katz, the science teacher, came over and joined us. Tony shook hands and Alan said with a smile, "You're lucky finding a job in any school today. This school always was one of the better schools but the last year or so, we have had a few problems that we never had before."

"What do you mean?" Jody asked.

"Unfortunately Judith, you'll find out," Alan said, "but let me explain some things to you now." I saw the warm look he gave Jody, as he took her arm and guided her to the back of the room where they sat together and talked.

Later, as we were drinking coffee, I asked Jody if I could drop her off at her apartment.

"Thanks, Michael," she replied, "but I just told Alan he could drive me home."

I sat there and watched the two of them leave, surprised at myself for feeling possessive of a girl I hardly knew. True, she was very desirable and there were bound to be men interested in her, I told myself quite logically. But that night lying in bed I couldn't get her out of my mind.

TWO

The Lascivious Teacher In The Bigoted School

Early the next morning I entered the school lounge which was filled with laughter as teachers who did not see each other over the summer exchanged hugs and kisses. My eyes scanned their faces as I tried to find Jody. Suddenly there she was and I could not take my eyes off of her.

She had the unique good looks that were a combination of a broad forehead and high cheek bones which were partially covered by a long, thick mass of auburn hair. Her almond-shaped blue eyes were set in a beautiful face which sparkled with animation as she spoke. Her wide full lips curved into a radiant smile that exposed flashing white teeth.

As I started to make my way through the crowded room to get to her, a thin striking blonde stepped in front of me. Laughing, she put her arm around me as she announced in a melodious, southern drawl to everyone.

"This is ah newest bachelor to join the Rowley Ranks, an as of now, ah put ma stamp on him!" Everyone grinned at each other, obviously used to this girl's antics.

"I'm Mary Ann, the music teacher, Michael. And ah come to make music in your homeroom three times a week. That's with all the pupils around so we don't have much time for privacy." She whispered in my ear. "But my apartments just around the corner from the school an anytime ya feel like coffee or anything at all just drop in."

Somewhat embarrassed by this girl's aggressive manner I smiled and said," excuse me, I have to speak to Judith before the bell."

"What are ya running over there for?" She asked with disdain.

"It would take a long hot summer to thaw her kind out." "But with me, you and I," she said teasingly, placing her hand on my arm "why even our names, Michael an Mary Ann, have a way ah melting together like a toasted cheese sandwich. Michael an Mary Ann, it sort of melts into one.

Did ya ever try ta pull apart ah hot, toasted, cheese sandwich?"

As Mary Ann talked, she seemed to have edged me into a corner of the room and I realized she was hungry for more than a toasted cheese! Her overt behavior in front of all the others repelled me. It was at this auspicious moment that Jody accidentally spilled her coffee which gave me a good excuse to get out of a "hot" corner.

I reached for some napkins and handed them to her so she could wipe her shirt.

"I guess I'm nervous about teaching the first day," she remarked, as we bent down to clean up the coffee from the floor.

"Don't be upset and don't worry," I told her. "All the teachers here got through a first day and we will, too."

She flashed that ravishing smile, "Thanks Mike. I needed that."

I followed her out to the hall as she commented, "It looks like Mary Ann really takes over the men."

"Maybe some," I said, "It depends what they're looking for. What I'm looking for is company on Friday after school. There's a lounge and eating spot that's popular with the teachers called 'The Black Dahlia', how about it?" "That sounds good to me, Michael." Just then the commanding voice of principal Bradshaw interrupted us. "The teachers rotate door duty every week,

Michael, and you're assigned for this first week of school."

"Assigned, you mean sentenced!" Alan Katz sneered, as he stood next to Jody.

I hurried to the entrance just as the bell rang. The tempo of the noise increased as a horde of boisterous teenagers entered from the playground, pushing and kicking one boy who wore a yarmulke and yelled "dirty Jew". Another boy picked up a fist to a black girl who was bused into this school and called her 'nigger'.

"O.K, boys, break it up, that's no way to talk in school or anywhere!" I yelled.

"Screw you'" they yelled at me, running off in different directions.

Alan shrugged and shook his head. "On door duty days it's better not to get up in the morning, Mike."

"Wow' Do they act like this every day?"

"Well, we have our share of vicious kids," Alan informed me.

All the while, Principal Bradshaw stood aside and listened without comment.

I wondered from his expression when he looked at Dr. Ling, the school psychologist and Alan Katz, what he was thinking.

He joined me as I walked to my classroom. Then he placed his hand tightly on my shoulder, obviously trying to suppress some inner conflict, and then he started to talk.

"Mike," he said slowly and deliberately, "seeing that you're my kind of young man, let me explain. He peered at me with an assuring glance which was meant to convey that this was a chat between friends. "Alan Katz and his buddy down there," he turned his head in the direction of Dr. Ling, "are obsessed with one word, minority. That pain in the ass, Katz, is a chronic complainer and that other one, Ling, continually disagrees with my philosophy. It would not be to your advantage to associate with them."

Instinctively, intuitively and instantly my loyalty went to Alan and Dr. Ling and I said angrily, "Those students had no right to get away with tormenting that Jewish boy or that black girl."

Principal Bradshaw gave me a solemn look. "Michael, they didn't really hurt those kids. They were just being bullies. We never have any real trouble here.

"But I don't think they should get away with bullying anyone!" I replied. "Michael, don't look for trouble. You make good money and have a nice

job here.

Being an Ancient History teacher you have the top students. Of course your homeroom has some disagreeable characters but so many young men like yourself are out of jobs now.

He paused and stared at me, and as far as he knew was getting his point across, falsely deluding himself about me.

"Teaching can be very simple or very difficult so my suggestion to you is see all, hear all, take your paycheck each week and have fun."

Bradshaw's words bothered me but as I entered my homeroom there was little time to think, as another half dozen rowdies upset the class with their swearing and yelling names at each other. Quickly I quieted them, took attendance and we saluted the flag but only three quarters of the students would pledge their allegiance.

Finally I sat down for our short meditation, which would hopefully afford me a moment of peace and quiet each day. After meditating, Louis Smith approached my desk.

"Mr. Ulrike," he started, "Do you know what I always think about when I meditate?"

"It's supposed to be private," I told him.

"Well," Louis said, "I'll tell you anyway. I asked God to punish all the people who don't let us have regular prayers in the school anymore!"

"Louis, you have to understand that our country's Declaration of Independence guarantees a separation of church and state. That is why we have to keep prayers and any form of religion out of the public school system. The public schools in America must uphold the laws of their land and not break them. Appearing to be satisfied with my answer, Louis walked back to his desk as Jody came by to give me her art schedule causing whistles and howls to fill the room.

"Don't forget we've got a date Friday after school." I whispered into her ear.

"I'll be sure and take care of that matter," she answered out loud, with a smile.

As she turned and walked away from me my eyes kept following the enticing sway of her hips. Her incredible body awakened those lusty desires in me until I was unhappily interrupted by the bell, which announced it was time for my Ancient History class to begin.

Friday after school I hurried downstairs to Jody's room which was a little storage area that had been built from a closet in the basement of the school. She poked her head out from behind some shelves.

"Welcome to my garret." she joked.

A painting with Jody's signature caught my eye and I recognized the portrait as one of my students.

"When did you do this oil painting?" I asked. "I painted it one night when I was home in my apartment. I paint from memory."

"Wouldn't you rather paint than teach?"

"Definitely, but I'd rather eat than starve." she answered with a laugh, as she walked over to me.

"Besides, my folks felt it was safer in a school with regular hours and regular pay, so here I am!" she said as she swung her bag over her shoulder and together we walked out of the building.

As I looked at her, I thought to myself how captivating she was with her long red hair pulled away from her face and knotted at the top of her head. The blue dress she wore accentuated her generous curves and allowed me the mental enjoyment of studying her many desirable and stimulating physical attributes.

"What are you staring at, Michael?"

"I'm admiring your beautiful mind, Jody." "Is that why you keep looking at my body?"

"You boggle my senses," I said, as I looked into her smiling blue eyes.

Just then we approached my car and Jody stopped short. A stricken look crossed her face as she pointed to the door.

"Look, look!" she gasped.

There, painted on the side of the car was a huge red swastika.

Shocked, but not wanting to upset her I said, "It must be those school kids acting up."

"It's more than kids acting up," she said angrily. "This kind of thing is going on everywhere lately." I knew her concern was well-founded, but I tried to make light of it so the evening wouldn't be ruined.

"Come on, get in the car." I said as I gave her a hand. "We can't solve this problem now," and I started the motor. I thought to myself about all the recent articles in the news concerning the growth of the Nazis and the KKK, but to Jody I only said, "The kids in this school will do anything to get a rise out of the teachers that's why all the walls are filled with graffiti. This is only another way of getting attention."

"Michael, I think your wrong, Most people are ignorant of history and don't realize that the hate of the Nazis and the Ku Klux Klan in today's world can cause a nuclear war and what's more"

She was ready to continue but I said, "Jody, we are going to put thoughts of the past out of our minds and not speak any further about the great

madness of the world! We are going to enjoy the evening ahead of us o.k.?"
She looked up at me, drew in a deep breath, and we both began to relax for
the first time in a week.

THREE

Night On The Town

The Black Dahlia was a large eating and drinking cafe with a four piece combo and a small dance floor. There was a wood-paneled lounge, with artificial hanging grape vines overhead that was big enough for tables of ten, yet lending itself to privacy for an intimate twosome. A large curved mahogany bar was crowded with people obviously well into their happy hour. The red and white checkered tablecloths, the scenic paintings of Venice on the walls and the delicious aromas suggested Italian food was their specialty. As Jody and I walked in we were greeted by Dr. Ling, the school psychologist, "Very welcome to honorable friends." He bowed from the waist, "Confucius say, 'He who join friends with drink on Friday, have 'weak end,' on Monday.'"

"That doesn't sound like Confucius to me, Dr. Ling."

"Michael, after four drinks and a week at the Rowley, my quotes come from confusion, not Confucius. Come, join us. Sit here next to Tony and his lovely wife, Cynthia. This next round of drinks is on me."

As we gave our orders to the waiter, Mary Ann sauntered up to our table. "What about me, ya all? Can't ah join over here in the fun?"

It was plain to see that neither Dr. Ling nor Cynthia was pleased with Mary Ann's intrusion, but the Doctor was a gentleman and invited her to have a drink.

"What is the lady's desire?" he asked.

"Ah have many desires. But ah have one real favorite drink, Southern

Comfort. Ah remember when ah first began to drink, ma daddy said, 'Mary Ann, don't drink anything except plain Bourbon, and ya never will get sick!' He should known cause he could drink anybody under the table. They didn't call him 'Iron Pots,' for nothing.

Mary Ann further informed us. "There's a new drink out that ya all should try.

It's called, The Fred Fud Pucker. It's a mixture of cranberry juice, vodka an Galliano."

Cynthia contemptuously ignored Mary Ann and turned to Jody asking, "How do you like the Rowley School?"

"It's not what I expected but I suppose I'll get used to it."

"My Tony's been there for nine years and he never got used to it." "How is it that he never transferred to another school?" Jody inquired naively.

"He has been trying for five years but right now with proposition two and a half, we're lucky he's got a job! Tony can't be too independent or fussy with four kids, mortgage payments on our house and car, and family health insurance to pay, and boy, do we ever need that with the kids!"

Mary Ann giggled as she turned to Tony, "What did ya go an have four kids for Tony, baby? Ah am sure your wife Cynthia Cohen De'Angelo, knows all the preventative measures!"

I quickly broke into the conversation, seeing where it may lead. "Come on, Jody, let's dance."

I had looked forward to holding this exquisite girl close to me ever since I first saw her. When I tightly enveloped my arms around her waist she rested her head under my chin and we moved slowly to the melodious love song, 'There's A Place In My Heart.' Without any effort she followed my steps, her body's rhythm completely in tune with mine. We pressed our bodies closer to each other and I could feel her breasts against my chest. The total awareness of Jody filled my being. Unexpectedly the mood changed and a fast beat permeated the air as we gyrated in all directions. On the last note I quickly pulled Jody to me and impetuously kissed her on the lips. I sensed by her response that we had affected each other equally.

The band retired for a rest and as we left the dance floor, Sylvia, the school speech therapist and her husband invited us to sit with them.

We declined, letting them know we were already sitting with others. As Sylvia looked over to our table she remarked,

"Oh, no, Cynthia and Tony are at the same table as "Hot Springs!""

"Who is Hot Springs?' Jody asked.

"Mary Ann," she gushed. "That means trouble! Mary Ann made a big play for Tony last winter and Cynthia really let her have it! Right after school in the parking lot there was a big fight! The language they used was unbelievable! It almost came to blows but instead of using their fists they swung their bags at one another. All the kids watched and yelled for their favorite teacher. Everyone knows Mary Ann craves men, in the plural.

They don't call her 'Hot Springs' for nothing. She is quite a tzatzkala. Now I guess she's got her eye on someone else. I'm surprised she hasn't made a play for a handsome guy like you Mike."

Jody gave me a questionable look as Sylvia kept talking. I couldn't help but wonder if her students in speech therapy ever had a chance to open their mouths.

Finally we broke away and went back to where we were sitting.

Mary Arm had been drinking all evening and was feeling no pain.

Suddenly she looked up at all the men present and announced loudly,

"Ah been sittin in this chair fa so long without dancing that ah got corns on ma ass!"

At this comment Cynthia gave Tony a push and they got up from their chairs, mentioned supper and the kids and quickly departed.

As time moved on, Mary Ann found herself a partner at the bar, and Alan left saying he had a date with a psychology major from Radcliff, who had some homework on sexual hang-ups and he was going to try and help her.

Friendly Dr. Ling kidded us as he waved goodnight and said,

"Teacher who befriend teacher, learn many things, if one be he and other be she."

Jody and I were now alone in the midst of many. We took a quiet table for two in the corner, lit the single candle in front of us and ordered a delicious Italian meal starting with an antipasto for two and some dry Chianti. We danced, talked and laughed until suddenly we were brought back to earth by a waiter who announced,

"This is the last round of drinks."

As we walked to the car there was a sudden chill in the air so I put my jacket over Jody's shoulders.

"I love the smell of your jacket." she said as she sniffed it." What cologne do you use?"

"I don't use cologne. That is me that you love." She gave me that dimpled smile of hers which made me stop the car on Memorial Drive. We got out and strolled arm in arm down the bike path on the Cambridge side of the Charles River. I kissed Jody softly, while across the water the giant buildings of the Hancock and the Prudential majestically rose above the city.

Further down the river the yachts, motor boats and other sailing vessels were tied to the dock. We laughed at some of the names on the ships. There was The Playmate, Promiscuous, Twice Spliced, and Sweet Miss—tress. I showed her M.I.T. which stretched impressively across from the river.

"I'd love to paint some of this scenery. Boston is beautiful!" she exclaimed. We went back to the car and she gave me directions to her apartment. "You live right around the corner from me Jody. I'm on Crescent and you're on Spaulding. Neighbor, you just got yourself limousine service to school from now on."

"That is wonderful. It's been a hassle getting some of my art equipment there by bus."

"You mentioned needing supplies for your pupils, Jody. One of these days I'm going into Cambridge to buy some pets to keep in my classroom. I could use your help."

"I would love to go with you. It is the least I can do after being offered limousine service."

Smiling, I said, "There will be a slight charge."

"Oh, that's all right, Michael. I'll chip in for the gas."

"I don't want you to spend your money on gas, Jody. I just want you to spend time with me."

The reflection of the moonlight shined on her beautiful face. I pulled her gently to me and felt her body tremble when we touched. Embracing her tightly I said,

"It feels so good to hold you in my arms. I kissed her closed eyes, her face and neck. My lips explored hers and the excited response of her kiss made me aware of my growing desire to possess her body.

"Michael, I think we better stop now," she murmured softly. "Stop what? We haven't done anything."

"But we could and we might." She answered.

I wiped my sweating brow and started the motor. After awhile Jody asked, "Do you still want me to go to Cambridge with you?"

"I still want to take you." I answered quietly.

As I drove her home I started to realize that my feelings for this girl were growing into something I never knew before.

FOUR

Cambridge

During the following weeks I saw Jody a great deal. One Saturday morning I picked her up to go into Cambridge. As she opened the car door I remarked, "We haven't been together for eleven hours. I've missed you." She looked at me and smiled but didn't reply.

Both of us were dressed in native costume, blue jeans, jerseys and sneakers.

But even this plain garb could not hide Jody's well endowed body and a long low whistle escaped my lips. Her thick red hair hung loosely over her shoulders, full and billowy in the breeze. The tight dungarees clung to her small waist and showed off her rounded hips.

She had a delightful rear end and I thought how nice it would feel to snuggle up to it.

But again, with all my mental strength I erased this thought from my mind.

Once in Cambridge we shopped for Jody's art supplies and then spent some time in the Harvard Coop, picking out records and poking through the book section.

"How about having a good cornbeef sandwich at the Wursthaus?" I asked.

"Ich esse gerne deutsche Gerichte." (I love to eat all German foods) she said.

After a delicious lunch at the restaurant, we found ourselves at Bailey's ice cream parlor where we enjoyed marshmallow, hot fudge sundaes.

Jody was staggered when I washed the sundae down with a double chocolate malted.

"Right now I'm addicted to food," I said laughing, "but I can see it wouldn't be hard to become addicted to you."

"Oh yeah?" she grinned, as I followed her out. Next we explored the health food store and came out loaded down with two large bags.

After putting them into the car we went to several pet shops and I bought a little brown hamster and a long-haired brown and white guinea pig that stole Jody's heart.

While driving to my apartment Jody lovingly vented her feelings about the little rodents.

"Michael, these little animals are just as wonderful and important in their way as we are in ours."

"That sounds like something my Grandfather would say." "What do you mean?" she asked.

"Well, for one thing, I wanted to go hunting when I was younger but he explained how inhumane it was."

"He sounds like a very kind man." Jody remarked.

"You would love him, everyone does. He is unusual, the most unusual person I have ever known'"

"Was he in the war?"

"Oh yes, from what he has told me in the past he had one of the most important commissions that there was. But my family won't talk about it. I guess the war was a real threat to them because they worked so hard in the underground. They all saw so much suffering, death and hate that now they just like to talk of the good life. I can't blame them."

We arrived at my apartment and carried the animals upstairs making them comfortable in the corner on the floor, when there came a soft rapping at my door.

"Michael, Michael, you are there?"

I opened the door and in walked my little, grey haired, spinster landlady,

I introduced Jody to Miss. Kravitz, who had lavished me with many kindnesses during the summer.

"Something for you I've made." She handed me a large dish.

"It is your favorite pineapple strudel that sweetens up your disposition." she laughed.

"But sweeter really he does not need to be, Jody." She patted my cheek. "And if I were fifty years younger under mine bed he could put the shoes anytime! With the beard even, a handsome man you can't hide. Neat and clean always he keeps his place."

Until this moment the animals in their cages had eluded Miss Kravitz but as she turned to leave, scratching noises from the animals brought her attention to the back of the room.

"Mice, mice in mine house?"

"Don't worry Miss Kravitz, I'm bringing them to school on Monday." "An ant, ah bug, a cockroach, never in mind house! Now, now, I got rats." I put my arm around Miss Kravitz, while Jody tried to comfort her.

"I promise you, Michael will keep them in their cages and Monday he will take them to school."

"That school's got plenty animals already! Mine own niece taught there one year only, then out she ran like from a fire. She went back to college and got her V.D. degree, and now in the college, future teachers, she teaches."

Laughing I said, "You mean she got her Ph.D. degree, Miss. Kravitz." "Well what ever, going I am now to bed, but sleeping I'm not! I am

thinking all night of mine house with the mice." She made a grimace.

"Thank you for the cake, Miss. Kravitz."

"It's not cake, Michael. It is strudel and don't give to the animals!" When she left, Jody helped me devour the pineapple strudel. "Hmmm, it is delicious! Can you make this?" I asked

"My mother is the artist in the kitchen." Jody replied.

We prepared supper in my big one room apartment. I started the coals on the hibachi while Jody tossed everything she could find into a salad. The cork popped, and we sat down on the couch to savor the wine and each other's company.

"Tell me Jody, do you have a boyfriend back in New York?"

"No, I don't have a boyfriend there. I have a good friend. His name is Bernie Goldberg, but I've known him for years.

"What about you?" she asked.

"Well back home there is Alice." I said "She's gorgeous, graceful and good at barn dancing, even though her legs don't coordinate too well."

"Oh?" She questioned.

Because of her disturbed look I quickly whispered in her ear. "Alice, is my horse."

I bent over and kissed her on the lips. We kissed longingly as I caressed her body.

For a brief moment her nipples became hard under my fingertips and a surge of desire overcame me, but Jody's hands grasped mine and in a thick emotional voice said,

"It's time for us to eat, Michael." I looked at her with longing, my body already pleasurably aroused, and sighed.

"You sure you want to eat now?"

"I'm kind of hungry. I hate to see the food burn." She said with conviction.

Later, after driving her home we stood at the door of her apartment and

I embraced her tightly.

"I'm in love with you Judith. Ich machte mit dir ins bett gehen." (You are very desirable and I would like to go to bed with you)

"Du macht es schwer zu widerstehen." she murmured. (You're making it hard to resist, Michael.)

"You don't have to resist Jody. I felt this way about you the first time I saw you. I wanted you then and I want you now."

"Michael, it's true that I am very attracted to you but we just met." And she gently pulled out of my arms.

"I have waited many years to feel the way I feel about you, Jody. Let's not spoil what we feel for one another."

At Jody's apartment the following week a phone call came in from her Mother in New York. They talked for awhile and I heard Jody mention going home. After she hung up she said, "My folks want me to come home for the Jewish holidays next week."

"Are you going?" I asked.

"Yes, they would be very disappointed if I didn't come for the holidays." "I will drive you to New York."

"No thanks Mike." A frown fixed itself upon her face and she became very quiet.

"Is there any special reason why I can't take you? Are you afraid I'll interfere with some of your personal plans?"

"No, of course not, it's just that if you really want to know and I don't mean to hurt you. It's my folks. They would be very upset because you're not of our faith."

"I'll only be driving you to New York Jody. What does that have to do with my being Jewish or not?"

"Well, they think that one thing leads to another and it's your background they would object to most because they suffered such brutality during the war in Germany. My parents told me that when my Father was only ten years old the Nazis came into his home in Germany and shot my Grandfather and tore my Father out of the arms of his Mother. Then they repeatedly smashed his right hand against a brick wall until it was crushed! He's had a stump for an arm ever since. He never saw his Mother again." She said as tears streamed down her face.

I put my arm around her and said, "I'm terribly sorry, Jody."

She continued speaking with thick emotion, "My Mother's parents and most of my aunts and uncles were gassed to death in the German concentration camps in Poland. Mother escaped when she was nine years old with her younger sister Frieda, and an old aunt. My Father managed to get away with another Jewish family."

"I can understand why they hate the Nazis, Jody, but there were Germans who tried to help the Jews, like my family. Some Germans lost their lives helping them escape.

But aside from all that Judith, I'm not a Nazi and my family was not Nazis! Is it what your folks will say that bothers you Jody, or is it you that is upset by my not being Jewish?

"Oh Michael, it's not that I'm so religious but if you were Jewish everything would be so much easier on my parents. Six million Jewish people were wiped out during the Second World War and we are a minority to begin with."

"Yes, I know Judith, and more Christians got killed in World War Two than in all the wars of history put together and that does not count the Japanese or the Chinese. Jody, we can't let the world's wrong doings interfere with the love we feel for one another." I held her in my arms and weighed in my mind how I could ever tell her that I had been a Priest.

FIVE

A Stranger Returns

Too soon the day arrived for Jody's holiday. The ride to the airport seemed much too short but the kiss goodbye was very long. I hated to see her go. I went back to my car wondering if her feelings for me would be changed when she returned.

The time dragged while she was away. My cousin Bob invited me to a party at his M.I.T. dormitory. It was like all the other parties I had gone to when I was in school.

The records blasted, the beer flowed and the girls were congenial but I found myself wondering, in the midst of it all, what Jody might be doing. I went out to the hall and called her in New York. A man's voice, with a German accent answered the phone.

"Is Judith there?" I asked. "Who's calling?" "Michael".

"Michael?

"Yes sir, Michael Ulricke"

There was no response from the other end. I thought we had been disconnected.

"Hello? Hello?"

The brisk voice answered back, I'll tell my daughter." I heard talking in the background and it was awhile before Jody's voice came over the wire.

"Hello Michael".

"Hi Jody, I didn't know when to pick you up at the airport."

"I'm taking the Eastern Airlines Shuttle Sunday night at eight thirty. "I should get in about nine twenty."

"I've missed you Jody."

"I hope it will be good flying weather." "Can't you talk?"

"I guess that's the way it is."

"I'll be waiting at the airport. It's been very lonesome without you Jody." "Bye, Mike."

As I put the receiver back, I wondered about her cool response.   I wondered if she had seen Bernie, her old home town boy friend. I wondered about a lot of things like the green-eyed jealous monster I saw in me. I guess I was going through that thing referred to in Paradise Lost as 'Lover's Hell'.

Nine o'clock Sunday night I was at Logan Airport having a drink in the Hemisphere Lounge, impatiently awaiting Jody's arrival. At nine-fifteen I grabbed my coat, leaving my unfinished drink on the table, and hurried to the shuttle gate. I spied that red hair and our eyes met. We ran toward each other and kissed, heedless of anyone around.

"Hey, 1 missed you, honey."

"I missed you too, Michael." she said softly. "You didn't sound that way over the phone."

"Well, I couldn't talk. Once my Father heard your last name he questioned me about you until I left."

"Let's get out of here." I said, as I led her to the car and drove off to her apartment.

Hurrying through the door, I dropped the suitcase to the floor as I wrapped my arms around her. I could feel the fast beating of her heart as I pressed her body closer to mine.

"Jody, I thought of you every night while you were away.

I kissed her lips and smothered by face into her long red tresses but I soon realized she was not responding in her usual way.

"I'm very tired from the trip, Michael, and the holidays and" "And I guess maybe I should leave." I said annoyed.

"Well, tomorrow is a work day." she replied.

"It never seemed to matter before." I said as I picked up my coat. "Want me to pick you up in the morning for school?"

"I'll be ready. Thanks Michael", she said as I walked down the hall.

I realized then, I should not have called her in New York. Her family was very important to her and whatever they had said obviously made a great impression on her. From that time on Jody started seeing Alan Katz frequently, and refused my every invitation.

SIX

The Ku Klux Klan

It wasn't until many weeks later that things changed between Jody and me. A few teachers and myself were outside in the students recreation area where the usual ball playing and yelling was going on and then, suddenly, we heard loud clapping and voices screaming, "WHITE POWER!", "WHITE POWER!"

The teachers quickly ran towards the back end of the yard where we saw about eight kids with white hoods covering their heads and faces. They were pushing two black boys and a small black girl into the corner of the schoolyard. The screams and clapping became louder and louder while others joined in yelling, "WHITE POWER!"

Immediately I rushed into the crowd of kids followed by the other teachers. The black children were down on the ground and the kids with the white hoods were hitting them with clubs. One black boy was hit on the head and started gushing blood.

"STOP IT! STOP IT!" I yelled as I pulled the clubs away from the two leaders, just before a third boy jumped on top of me and tried to hit me with his club.

Although he was larger, I managed to get him down on the ground and free myself long enough to get a good hold of him while Tony ripped off his white hood. All at once there was a silence, as the other teachers helped the black children up and carried the bleeding boy Edgar, into the school to await the ambulance.

"What's the meaning of this? What's going on?" yelled Principal Bradshaw as he came running towards us.

The boy I was holding shook himself free of my hands and answered the principal.

"Those niggers don't belong in our school! We don't want them colored kids bused into our part of town! Let them go to school where they live!"

What are you wearing white hoods for?" I asked him. "We are the Ku Klux Klan! And there ain't no law against it!" He yelled at me, as he spit out of the side of his mouth. His gang clapped and whistled at his remarks and he continued,

"We got a right to be an all white school if we want an all white city if we want an all white state if we want and an all white country if we want without no niggers or Semites! My father says so and he's right! We don't want mixed people just pure Aryans!"

"You tell them Eric!" A boy's voice yelled from behind me.

"Break it up you kids! Cut out this riot and report to my office! "Principal Bradshaw roared.

As everyone started to go inside I asked Bradshaw.

"What do you intend to do about this, this hatred that seems to be running rampant in your school?"

"It's not, as you put it running rampant. All kids break out fighting every now and then. I suggest you keep out of it Michael. The less we make of it the better. We can't stop the way kids feel, so there is very little we can do." he said in an off hand manner.

"Remember, it's a democracy we live in Michael people have rights and don't you forget it!"

"'This may be a democracy but it's not democratic of you, a principal, to let any of the students have a right to endanger the life of another student. The incidents in this school can snowball and you don't know where they will end!

This Ku Klux Klan is an organization that parallels with the Nazis. They have a talent to hate and they use it against the Catholic, the Jew,

the black, the Indian, the Chinese, the Muslim and more!" I said angrily.' "You don't really think these kids are part of the KKK!" Bradshaw said

as he laughed.

"Don't laugh Mr. Bradshaw. They are not a joke!

The Ku Klux Klan starts training their Klan Youth Corps at the age of ten and they teach them to use guns and rifles! That's why there has been a new project launched called Klanwatch, by the Southern Poverty Law Center. It fights the growth of Klan violence and intimidation."

"But that's only in the south, Michael."

"Can't you see it's moving all over the country Mr. Bradshaw, or do you have the myopia of the masses? Why do you think some politicians worked so hard to get the platform of the Democratic Party to condemn the Klan and its activities?

I think you ought to have a meeting about this. Let the Civil Liberties Union know what's happening here before someone really gets hurt."

"Don't tell me how to run my school, Michael! These kids aren't learning these things here and they all come from fine families. In fact, Eric's father was just elected to the city council."

"What does that have to do with the actions of these boys, Bradshaw?"

Getting angrier by the moment I said, "The fact is that the minds of these kids are poisoned and since they don't learn it in school and since they come from what you call, 'fine families,' where do they learn it? You heard what Eric said, his father told him!"

"I'll talk to these troublemakers in my office and they will be kept after school."

That's not enough Bradshaw. This school is infested with bigots and it's getting worse! You've got to speak to the parents and get help from the school board.

Do something!"

"I'm not making a big deal over this. It will pass. I don't want any committee meetings. It will only make my school look bad."

"Your school looks bad anyway and if that black boy Edgar dies, it will be in every newspaper in the country!"

I looked Bradshaw in the eyes as I said, "I'm telling you now, if you won't make an appointment with the school board, I will!"

"Go Michael, see all the committees you want just leave me out of it!" he bellowed as he walked away.

"You're in it Bradshaw! You're the principal here!" I yelled disgusted with this man who wanted to remain, uninvolved. It was at this moment that I heard Jody call my name and as I turned around I saw her behind me.

"I heard what you said, Michael. You were wonderful, the way you told off Bradshaw! I hope you're going through with a committee meeting."

"Of course I am! It's outrageous to have children terrorizing other children in a public school. Hate has covered the world with blood to our time, but this time it can be worse than ever before. The Nazis, the Ku Klux Klan and other powerful groups in a world of nuclear weapons and missiles can lead us to only one place if"

"Michael, calm down!" she said as she put her hand on my arm, "I never realized you had such strong convictions. You remind me of my Father." she smiled up at me and asked, "Want to drive me home after school?"

SEVEN

Sea Shells Of Rockport

During the weeks that followed, Jody and I spent all our spare time together and Alan Katz, became a part of her past.

After school one afternoon, on one of those beautiful Indian summer days, unique to New England, Jody and I drove off toward the North Shore. The beauty of the autumn countryside was everywhere around us. The sky was clear blue overhead and the trees were ablaze in flaming scarlet, reds and gold. Along the roadside amethyst chrysanthemums had burst into bloom. We stopped by the side of the road to take pictures and I captured the mood of the season which was evident in the glow that radiated from Jody's face. Her flaming red hair blended perfectly with the foliage, and passers-by stopped and looked admiringly in her direction.

After touring Gloucester, Pigeon Cove and Annisquam, we finally stopped in Rockport, which is one of the most charming sea towns in New England. Here in Rockport, New England saltbox homes had been converted into antique shops and art galleries. The combination of fishing village, gift shops and art colony drew people here from all parts of the world.

We strolled along Bearskin Neck and Tuna Wharf admiring the beautiful crafts and works of art from native artists and other countries.

In Ipswich Bay we watched the fishermen come in with their catch and listened to the seagulls announce that suppertime had come.

At one of the seaside restaurants we had chowder and lobster sandwiches and for a while we sat on the boulders of Marinion Way watching the foamy surf splash against the rocks. The sun sank behind the horizon and we took off our shoes and walked along the water's edge.

It was becoming dark and the beach was deserted as we sat down and dug our toes into the soft, warm sand. A chilling gust of wind swept over us as I enclosed Jody, close and warm in my arms. The desire to make love to her was very strong within me, but I listened to my head instead of my heart which told me, 'take it easy and take it slow'. I bent over and picked up a beautiful seashell and held it to her ear.

"Listen, it has a secret to tell. It says, 'Ich liebe dich liebchen' (I love you sweetheart) and there on the sands I drew her to me and we kissed each other longingly, as the waves splashed against our legs.

She clung to me and her whole body trembled as I held her tight. She looked up into my eyes, touching my face with her fingertips,

"Michael, I didn't know love could happen like this. Just a few weeks ago I didn't know you existed and now we're a part of each others lives. It's almost like a dream. Hold me Michael, kiss me. Make love to me."

There in the darkness of the empty moonlit beach I fumbled to open the buttons of her shirt. I caressed her soft, warm full breasts as she pushed her body closer to mine. Every part of me cried out for her. We had made love hundreds of times in my imagination, but now her inexperience made her even more desirable to me. She waited, wanting me as I wanted her. With complete abandonment the clothes dropped from our bodies and we moved together to the tempo of one, oblivious to the outside world.

The throbbing rhythm within us grew greater and greater, with each roll of the tide. We touched and explored each other ecstatically. I tried to be as gentle and as tender as I could but she cried out. I started to pull away but her arms tightened around me and we reached the magical wonder of physical love. A beautiful woman came to life.

I looked down at her. "Are you alright?" There was love in her eyes as she softly murmured, as if in a dream, "Michael, I never knew anyone could feel like this."

"You've found out what it is to be a woman Jody." "It's a wonderful thing Michael, being a woman."

"That's only part of it". I said. "It's you and me, together with love that makes it as wonderful as this."

"I love you, Michael."

"And I love you Jody, now and forever." Contented, we lay together on the sand and listened to the tide as we watched the moon smile down at us. We had no premonition that our lives were under the shadow of a very dark cloud.

EIGHT

Celibacy

There were many parties around the school which Jody and I had not attended. We felt happy just being alone together. This particular afternoon, as we stopped to read the poster in the cafeteria about the hospital dinner dance, to be held at the main ballroom of the Sheraton Regis, Tony came over. "How

about joining us?" He asked referring to the poster.

"Everyone's going. It's the big event of the year and besides we very rarely get to see you two socially. We'll even pick you up."

"Sounds like fun Michael and it's a worthy cause." Jody added.

We all agreed and Tony said he would pick us up at six sharp Saturday night.

Jody mentioned she would need to shop for a gown and asked me to go with her. So the following afternoon we drove out of the school parking lot and headed for Boston as the kids yelled, "Have a good time, teach."

At the first store on Newbury Street, Jody spotted a gown in the window that caught her eye.

"Come on, let's go in and you can try it on." I said. "Michael, that gown will cost me a months salary!" "Well, let's just see what it looks like on you."

A saleslady with a French accent greeted us and Jody pointed out the gown in the window.

"You are very, very lucky. The one in the window it is just your size. It is an original." A moment later someone took the elegant white peau de soie gown off the mannequin. It had tiny gold threads and small seed pearls woven into the material.

The saleswoman went into the fitting room with Jody and on her return remarked,

"That gown, it was truly made to order for her. It is a perfect fit! Your wife, she is a beauty anyway. Just wait until you see her in this gown!"

Little did this woman realize that when she called her 'my wife' it upset me because marriage is what Jody refused to discuss. She evaded every overture I made in reference to it.

Just then Jody walked towards us, everyone in the shop turned to look. "Do you like it, Michael?" she asked sparkling. The total effect was overwhelming.

"Yes, indeed I do."

"Your wife she fills it out perfectly. She looks like a reigning beauty. I would not change a single thread. The length, the fit, it is perfect. I could use her for a model in my shop." she said in her heavy French accent.

As Jody walked back to the fitting room, I quickly made out a check and gave it to the saleswoman. Later Jody was reticent about my having paid for it.

"It's a birthday gift." I assured her. "But my birthday isn't here yet."

"It's for all the birthdays when I didn't know you." I whispered. The saleswoman handed the box to Jody.

"Enjoy ze gown Mrs.Ulricke."

Jody looked at me pensively and a slight frown crossed her face. "Where would you like to go now Mrs. Ulricke?" I asked smiling as I opened the car door for her.

"Home sir, I am making ze dinner for us." she laughed. "What ever you desire Mrs. Ulricke." I joked.

"You may as well get used to the name Jody, because people are taking it for granted like the saleswoman, the whole school, everyone except you."

"Michael, please, I need time."

.I looked at her as we drove along. You can have all the time it takes. You just have to make up your mind if you love me enough to marry me."

"Michael, don't put it that way!"

"That's what it comes down to, Jody. You're the one who has to decide, not your family. And as long as we are mentioning 'family', you may as well know a little more about mine. I don't think I mentioned to you that for awhile we had a clergyman in our family, but then he decided he was not cut out for that kind of life."

"You had a priest in your family? That's one part of the Catholic religion I could never understand Michael, why priest's should practice celibacy. It's really unfortunate that some of the most intelligent and handsome priests, who should be husbands and fathers and perpetuate the best of everything do not have children."

"Those are exactly my sentiments. I'm glad you agree with me." I smiled to myself as I thought about the days when I had just left the priesthood and had dated many beautiful, exciting and intelligent girls. But suddenly, this girl eclipsed all the others making a lasting impression in the very depths of my soul. I had found in her the warmth, the mental communication, and gentle nature of a very sensitive human being. Everything I wanted in a woman was in Jody. It was she I wanted in my home as mother to the children that I never thought I would have. Until now, I had been reluctant to tell her about my having been a priest, since I knew her feelings about our being of different faiths was very upsetting to her. But, our growing affection and devotion to each other committed me to explain to her this experience in my life. Saturday night at the dance, I would tell her. I did not want our relationship to remain only an arrangement.

That evening, after dinner at her apartment I reached for her hand across the table. "This is my dessert." I said as I lifted her hand to my lips. She moved towards me and the sweet smell of her awakened my senses. I fondled her breasts one by one as we moved together toward the bedroom. My fingers pressed into the soft flesh of her body, and I paced myself by her tender sighs of pleasure. I lifted my body so that we could move in unison, and as her soft warmth surrounded me I knew I was securely in place.

It was then I felt that pleasurable tingle that does not exist anywhere else in life. It was that incredible bond of bliss. I tried to prolong the ecstasy for us but as Jody tightened her legs around my body, we felt that 'need' with every fiber of our being.

Our hips heaved, our bodies swayed and for one precious moment we remained on the Summit, until we burst into the final culmination of our love.

"It felt so good Michael."

"That's what love does. It gets better each time." "That's what love means to you Michael?"

"No. It doesn't just mean a good sex life. It means sharing and caring for each other.

Wanting to be with each other and having a future as husband and wife." "Michael, now you're bringing me back to reality." She said as she sat up in bed.

"Most girls after going to bed with a guy would be very happy to hear him talk about love and marriage, unless of course, they don't love"

"Oh Michael, of course 1 love you. It's just that if we married there would be such problems."

"You're talking about your folks being upset when we marry." "It isn't 'when' Michael, it's 'how'."

"Why should it be such a problem when we're so good together?" I asked as I put my face down to kiss her breast once again. She jumped off the bed. "Michael, don't confuse the issue. We have a problem, and we may as well talk about it."

"All right, Jody, what would you suggest? Maybe we should just have a sexy inter-religious relationship for awhile, and see how it works out." I said teasingly.

"We could." Jody answered.

"You would agree to something like this, instead of marriage?" I asked, stunned.

"I think it's the only way right now, Michael. Gradually, in time, my parents will get to know you and like you, but right now if I told them I was marrying out of my faith they would be heartbroken."

As I listened to her words I felt more and more like a traitor not telling her about by past in the priesthood. I looked at this girl who I loved and I was fearful of losing her. The timing was not right but as the week progressed I made up my mind to tell her at the dinner dance, and then hopefully slip an engagement ring on her finger.

NINE

The Truth

As I dressed for the hospital affair, I fortified myself with arguments that I hoped Jody could not break down. Putting, on my white dinner jacket, I straightened my tie in the mirror, put the jewelry box into my pocket and drove to her apartment. With great expectations for the evening I entered the building and hurried toward the elevator, where a tall, well dressed, smiling young man held the door open for me. Reaching Jody's floor, the same good looking man brushed past me in great haste. Then to my surprise he stopped a short distance ahead of me at Jody's door, and rang the bell. Immediately the door opened and his loud jovial greeting filled the air.

"Hey, Jody baby!"

"Bernie, what are you doing here?" Without answering he grabbed her quickly by the waist and hugged her. Then moving her back at arms length into the apartment he exclaimed, "You look sensational, kid!" He put his arms around her obviously intending a serious kiss. At this moment Jody looked up from him and saw me standing in the doorway.

"Mike, I didn't see you out there." she said, pulling out of Bernie's arms. This is Bernie Goldberg, an old friend from New York. Michael is from Maryland. He teaches Ancient History in my school," she said as we walked

into her apartment.

Bernie smiled broadly and we shook hands as he commented,

"I go to Maryland almost every week on legal business. A client of my law firm, The Dreyfus Paper Company, is there. In fact, I keep my yacht harbored at their club since I'm there so much in the summer. Fishing, that's the life! Do you fish, Mike?"

"Not lately." I said.

"Jody and her family have been on my boat a few times and we've had great times.

Isn't that right, Jody?"

There was no reply and I concentrated on lighting my pipe. Bernie made himself comfortable in the big chair, putting his feet up on the ottoman and started smoking his cigar.

"How about having a drink?" Jody asked.

"I don't want to hold you people up. You look like you're dressed for a special occasion." He remarked.

"We have a hospital dinner dance tonight but we have time for a drink, don't we, Michael?" Jody asked as she disappeared into the kitchen to mix cocktails.

I followed close at her heels.

"What is he doing here tonight, Jody?"

"I don't know. I didn't know he was coming. He surprised us both."

She put her arms around me and I kissed the side of her neck while I whispered, "You look exquisite tonight. You'll be the belle of the ball, if we ever get there."

She carried the tray of drinks into the living room and as we sipped our cocktails I watched Bernie's eyes which followed Jody's every move. The scoop neckline of her dress outlined her full breasts and Bernie's concentrated stare indicated interests other than brotherly love.

"By the way, Jody," Bernie remarked, "your folks send their love. I saw them before I left."-

As he talked he took out an envelope from his pocket and handed it to Jody.

"I was supposed to mail this to you but I used it as an excuse to come up and see you. It's from the Manhattan Art Association."

"Oh, I hope this is good news." she said.

"Open it and see," he encouraged her. As she opened the envelope she jumped up from the couch.

"Oh, my goodness I won! I won!" "What did you win?" I asked. "I'll read it to you.

'Dear Miss. Loeb,

We are very pleased to inform you that your oil painting of, 'The Market Place,' has won third prize in our New York Art Exibition. We have enclosed a check for five hundred dollars. Good luck in your future endeavors. Best Regards, Franklin Todd, President, Manhattan Art Association.'

"'1 can't believe it!" she said

"I knew you could do it." Bernie praised her. "Congratulations, you're really a professional now."

"How long ago did you send in the painting?" I asked.

"Michael it was so long ago that I had completely forgotten about it."

"I can guarantee you," Bernie said confidently, "that if you came back to New York Jody, within six months, with your talent and my connections you would be one of the most sought after new young artists in the city!" Judith hesitated.

"It's a very flattering thought but I wouldn't want to leave now."

"The way teachers are looking for jobs nowadays," Bernie remarked, "they can replace you overnight. Isn't that right, Mike?"

"Well, Judith is a mighty fine teacher. It is true that many teachers are looking for jobs but it's hard to get a teacher as good as Jody."

Bernie's possessive and domineering manner towards Jody was beginning to make me angry. They appeared to have known each other for quite a long time. He was obviously successful and his religious background was the same as Jody's. A man her family could easily accept. Doubts began tugging at me when three rings on the downstairs buzzer gave us the signal that Tony and Cynthia were waiting.

"That's for us. We have to leave now," Jody said. As Bernie put his coat on I heard him say to her,

"I'll call you tomorrow about noon."

"That's fine Bernie and thanks so much for bringing that letter to me." "Nice meeting you Bernie." I said as I quickly opened the door for him

to leave. After he had gone I turned to Jody. "Are there any more at home like that one?"

"Oh Michael, Bernie and his folks have been wonderful friends through the years. His father grew up with mine in Germany and is the surgeon who operated on my father's arm that was destroyed by the Nazis, giving him better mobility with the shoulder.

"I didn't know that." I said

"But he's only a friend and besides they're waiting for us downstairs."

We walked out of the building and got into Tony's car as Bernie drove past us and waved. Cynthia immediately asked,

"Jody, who in the world was that handsome Adonis waving goodbye to you from that gorgeous, silver grey Lincoln Continental?"

"He's an old friend of the family from back home."

"Friends like that ought to stay in New York, right Mike?" Tony winked in the car mirror. I made no reply and Jody looked up at me and whispered, "Michael, please don't let Bernie spoil our evening, especially when we

can celebrate my winning the contest." As we talked about Jody's good luck Bernie was forgotten and the gay 'night out' atmosphere filled the car as we drove along.

The doorman at the hotel took care of the parking and we walked into the crowded ballroom. It was filled with beautifully coiffed women, their fragrant perfumes filled the air as they swished by in their long silk and chiffon gowns. People had gathered in small groups drinking and talking. I squeezed Jody's hand and said, "Everybody's looking at you."

"Oh, a little paint makes ya what ya ain't." She said in a frivolous mood. Friendly faces floated past, from time to time stopping to talk as we sat at our table with Cynthia, Tony, Dr. Ling and a few others. We danced the first dance together and Judith nuzzled her soft face into the nape of my neck. I embraced her tightly, trying to obscure from my mind, 'The New York Intrusion", but annoyed that Bernie was planning to call Jody tomorrow. We moved effortlessly across the enormous ballroom with the strains of Cole Porter's, 'Embraceable You.' I hummed in her ear, 'I love all the many charms about you, most of all I love my arms about you." Jody looked up smiling and then shook her head and said, "Here comes, Hot Springs."

I looked up to see Mary Ann in a gold lame jumpsuit dancing over to us with Alan Katz.

"Hi there, ya all. Are ya havin ah good time? We have ah seats at the very next table from you Michael, an I am savin a few dances especially for you! Now don't ya forget about me. By the way, ya look absolutely divine in ya white dinner jacket Michael."

As we danced away Jody mimicked Mary Ann, "Ya look positively devine in ya white dinner jacket an ah am savin a few dances especially for ya!"

"Come on now Jody, she's only fooling around."

"I don't think so Michael. I think she is one girl with an awful lot of 'chutzpah'."

"What's that mean?"

"It means, nerve, plain old fashion nerve!"

The music stopped and we sat down at our table. Dr. Ling lifted his glass and remarked,"

"You both looked radiant on the dance floor. Love is in the air. A certain glow is everywhere."

"Dr., you always have a rhyme for everything." Jody told him.

"That's because I'm Dr. Ling, but I only say the nicest things." He smiled while everyone laughed. People started drifting back to their tables and the delicious aroma of succulent roasted lamb, rice pilaf, salad and buttered squash filled the air.

As we started eating our fruit cup, my eyes lifted and the unexpected sight of a huge bulk of a man rushed past me and stopped a few tables away from ours. His slightly balding hairline made his unusual broad forehead even more prominent. Something about him looked familiar. Those large flashing black eyes could only belong to one human being in the world! Charles Buono, my former Seminarian Brother, who had been in the same Parish as me. My first instinct was to get up from my chair and rush over to him, when I caught myself and sat down again. Jody's eyes met mine.

"Where are you going Michael?"

"I'm not going anywhere, Jody." This is a nice fix, I said to myself, becoming very uneasy knowing Charles would see me at any moment. I stopped eating.

"Michael, what is the matter with you? You're not eating!" "I guess I don't have much of an appetite."

"But you always have an appetite. Is there something wrong?" "Je suis tomber dans le panneau." (I'm about to fall into a trap) "What's that Michael?"

"Only that whatever happens Jody, remember I love you very, very much." "I know you love me Michael," she whispered, "and I love you too but why are you so serious all of a sudden? Maybe a drink with your friends at

the bar would make you feel better."

As I started to get up from my seat, Charles walked past me, stopped, turned around to our table, raised his arms and rushed over and embraced me.

"Michael! Michael Ulricke! What are you doing here?"

"Charles Buono," I said, "1 haven't seen you in"

"In four years, Michael, since you and I left the parish. Michael, how are you? Are you still keeping the faith?"

"Charles, things have changed quite a bit with me."

"I am sure they did. You must be living a completely different life since you were a priest. I know I am."

I turned to see Jody look at me with a shocked expression. The color had drained from her face. Without saying a thing and before I could explain, she got up and fled from the room.

"Is that gorgeous girl with you Mike?"

"Yes, but there are some things I've neglected to tell her about myself and right now I think she is very upset."

"Well if she is as wonderful as she is beautiful you better go after her."

I started after Jody but was intercepted by Mary Ann, who stood in my path smiling.

"Oh Mike, ah heard what your friend Charles here said. It absolutely saddled ma syncopation! Ah just couldn't believe my ears. You were a Priest?"

Charles then took Mary Ann's hand,

"Little lady, anytime you need to confess anything at all let me help you.

I've had lots of experience."

"Well, ah do confess that ah can't understand why so many verile looking men prefer having nocturnal emission ta going ta bed with a woman!"

Again I started after Jody but she had entered the lady's room. As I stood and waited outside the door Tony came over and patted me on the back saying,

"Here Mike, take my car keys, we'll get a ride with someone. Good luck!" Several minutes later Jody rushed past me. I followed close behind her,

"Jody!" I yelled

"I don't want to say anything I'll be sorry for, Michael. Why, why didn't you tell me about yourself?"

"Why should it make such a difference Jody? I'm still me. I haven't changed."

"But you weren't honest with me. You know my feelings!" "You're right Jody, I should have told you."

"You deceived me!"

"Not on purpose. I planned on telling you at the right time but I was afraid of your reaction."

"I don't want to talk about it anymore Michael. You don't care about what I feel or about what I think. What difference does it make now anyway?" she asked.

"What you think makes a big difference to me Jody. I love you."

"I'm, I'm all mixed up." she blurted out. "I've got to be alone and sort things out in my mind. Maybe we shouldn't see each other for awhile. Let me think."

Feeling angry with myself we drove home in silence. Hoping to talk, I stopped the car in front of her apartment house and turned off the ignition, but she hastily jumped out of the car and ran into the building leaving me alone in the dark with my thoughts.

Once home and unable to sleep I dialed Jody's number. There was no answer.

Many times during the night I called but no one picked up the phone. Toward the wee hours of the morning I dozed off from sheer weariness but intermittently awoke from a restless sleep and dialed again. Why wasn't she there? Was she home and not answering?

If she wasn't there would she have been with Bernie? Did something happen to her?

All sorts of unpleasant thoughts crossed my mind. The next morning I called Tony to tell him I was bringing over his car keys. He told me Cynthia had spoken to Jody and had learned she was going home to New York. During the week that followed I telephoned New York many times. Jody's Father's brisk voice always informed me that she was not there. Finally I sat down and wrote a letter to her that I hoped would explain the many things I had not been able to tell her.

Dearest Jody,

Having spent almost a week not seeing or hearing from you has hurt me more than words can describe.

The mistake I made by not telling you of my having been a priest was because I was afraid, yes afraid of losing you.

I realized it was upsetting to you that I was not of your faith. Knowing this I felt if I told you right away about having been a priest it might cause the end of our relationship altogether, and so, I kept waiting for the right time, the right time which never came.

Before I met you it became obvious to me that your people and mine have been torn apart by certain religious ideas that have been misunderstood for thousands of years.

Please don't let these misunderstandings tear us apart now.

I love you very much Judith, and if you love me as I feel you do, we cannot let these problems from the past interfere with our chance for happiness.

Always, Michael

But there was no answer from Jody.

TEN

Her Lust To Learn

A week had past since the dinner dance and as I lay in bed taking advantage of Saturday morning and thinking of Jody, there was a knock at the door. I looked at the clock. It was one in the afternoon. I couldn't believe I had slept this late. The knocking continued and I thought to myself hopefully, maybe it's Jody. Maybe she thought it all over and came back. I jumped out of bed and opened the door to find Mary Ann standing in the hall, holding a bottle of wine.

"Michael ah felt that for many years you have listened with a sympathetic ear as a priest but today you need someone ta help you. Ah want ta be with ya at this time."

With these words she walked into my apartment, uninvited.

"Ah baked a little cake but ah see ya didn't even have breakfast, so I'm going ta whip ya up a little something. Now just do whatever ya have ta do and don't mind me."

"That's very nice of you Mary Ann but really I don't think I'm in the mood to eat."

"Don't be silly! Men are always hungry. Some are hungry for one thing and some are hungry for another thing. I want you should know I am a very good cook and ya won't be able ta resist me!"

"Well make yourself comfortable if you want. I'm going to take a shower." Hopefully the brisk, cold water would make me feel better, and all this week would disappear like a bad dream from which I would soon awake. But when the bathroom door opened and I saw Mary Ann poke her blonde head through the door, I knew I was awake.

"Peek-a-boo, ah see you. Ah have a delicious breakfast ready an ah have a delectable dessert waiting." As she turned around I noticed that under her apron she was completely nude.

"Mary Ann," I yelled to her, "I'm not very hungry and I know I won't want dessert."

When I came out of the bathroom Mary Ann did have a delicious breakfast of eggs, pancakes and coffee on the table and thank goodness all her clothes were back on.

"Ah don't believe any man should lose his appetite because some spoiled Jewish American Princess thinks she is too good fa him! Jody knew you were a Catholic Michael. Just because she found out ya once was a priest she didn't have ta get so upset an go running back ta New York. Michael, let's talk about it,"

"There is nothing to talk about Mary Ann."

"You probably just fell in love with her looks Michael. Ah bet she had a nose job and wasn't really born that pretty! Besides, if she really loved ya she would have waited ta hear why ya didn't tell her before about being a priest an why ya gave it up. Why did ya give it up, Michael? Was it because ya weren't allowed a sex life? Did ya have a girl ya were in love with? Why didn't ya want ta be a father, Michael?"

"Oh, I decided I wanted to be a father, Mary Ann, but a father to my own children, along with a wife I could love. My education certainly was not wasted, in fact, the more I studied and read about the different religions the more interested I became in them. I discovered they all shared the same deep-rooted faiths and superstitions way back over forty thousand years ago, something that very few people know about today."

"What do you mean?" Mary Ann asked. "Are you really interested?"

"Oh yes, yes ah am! Ah am opening ma mind."

"Over forty thousand years ago, long before there were any nations, thousands of stone age tribes roamed the wastelands of Arabia, Western Asia and Africa. These pre-historic tribes gave birth to beliefs that became the basis from which religion stemmed.

"Oh, ah know the Commandments Mike. An ma religion is very important ta me, especially confession. Confession works like ah suppository fa ma soul!

An besides ah have a priest that is a doll! He is ma confidant for years, and if ah didn't have him ah would end up payin a psychiatrist ta hear me disembowel ma mind. It would cost me a fortune!" she said breathlessly. "Now ma soul is saved fa practically nothin!"

"Mary Ann, just what is your soul being saved for?"

"Well, right now ah can't think of anything. But ah do know what ah am saving ma body for!" She gave me a wink and laughed, and then in a more serious tone said.

"What man really needs is to be closer to his fellow man. Ma daddy always quoted the Bible, just like you, Mike. We all learned from daddy as we grew up. He said that in Malachi, chapter two, line ten, it asks, 'Have we not all one father? Hath not one God created us? Why do we deal treacherously every man against his brother, by profaning the covenant of our fathers?' Yes, daddy was right we do need to be closer to ah fellow-man!"

I absently-toyed with my coffee cup as Mary Ann walked behind my chair and started running her fingers through my hair. She bent over and kissed me on the neck and whispered in my ear.

"Ya know Mike, if ah were in Jody's place ah wouldn't leave ya, not for a moment! You are such ah intelligent, unusual human being. Ya seem ta be so interested in cultivatin ma mind. Most young men in your place would only be interested in fooling around with ma body! Ah have never met anyone as wonderful as you before!"

I stood up, "One day Mary Ann the right man will come along and you will feel that way about him." Mary Ann put her arms around me and laid her blonde head on my shoulder.

"Michael, the right man has come along. I'm not about to hide it.' I'm in love with ya Mike. Ah know ya don't love me and it's alright. Ah just want us to be happy now. Ah just want ta be near ya. Ah just want ya to hold me close. Ah need ya Mike. Ah need ya ta hold me. Ah am so alone."

"Mary Ann," I said as I held her away from me by the shoulders, "You're a beautiful young woman and many men could fall in love with you."

"Any man but you!" she cried, throwing herself down on the couch. "Ah suppose ya secretly hoping Jody will call ya and say she forgives ya, but Mike she has already forgotten all about ya." "What do you mean Mary Ann?"

"Neva yà mind what I mean. She's just been leading ya on." "What makes you, think so?"

"Well if ya must know, she already has a boyfriend from New York! When ah drove by her apartment building last Sunday she was getting into ah silver grey Continental with New York number plates and a handsome fella was driving.

I suddenly felt hollow as I thought to myself, Bernie had won!

"Mike, ah hope ya not angry with me for what I said bout Jody, but I feel ya aught ta know. An besides, there are times when we need friends ta help us out of a situation." Mary Ann sat down beside me on the couch and patted my head trying to calm me.

I was at a loss for words. She leaned against me for a moment and held me tight. It was then I felt her hand slowly moving inside my shirt. As I tried to get up she cried cut and pulled me down beside her. Before I realized what was happening she tore open her shirt and covered my face with her naked breasts. The next instant they were in my mouth.

In an urgent frenzy she pulled down my zipper and climbed on top of me. Her magic fingers moved up and down. I felt an ecstatic sensation and couldn't push her away. She was so warm, so soft, so loving. I savored each moment as my sensuality increased.

"It feels so good Mike, so good," she murmured as the throbs increased and we rode the hills, the valleys and the swift-flowing stream with wild uncontrollable lust. Later that night Mary Ann asked,

"Michael, let me stay with you, if you decide you don't want me anymore I'll go. It was so good between us. I could make you feel that way all the time Michael. You liked it. You know you did. You can't deny that!"

"Mary Ann, something came over us both tonight. It's no ones fault, but my mind is too unsettled right now and it wouldn't be fair to you." We both dressed and I helped her on with her coat as she remarked, "Mike someday, somewhere if ya want me just remember, I'll be there!" Without another word she quickly walked out of my apartment.

I threw myself into a chair and though what a mess I had made of everything. The next morning on my way back from picking up a newspaper the face of my little old landlady peeked out of her door.

"Michael, I got for you some delicious challah. Just now, out from mine oven it came."

She asked me to join her for a cup of tea and I gladly accepted.

"I'm glad you invited me to stop in Miss. Kravitz. I could use someone to talk to right now."

"Something is bothering you Michael? Maybe you have a little girl trouble?"

"Yes, it's Jody trouble. Do you remember when I first moved in here? I showed you my credentials and told you I had been a priest but had given it up."

"I remember. Then a long talk we had about religion and I said, no difference did it matter to me as long as a good human being you are. So, about this trouble tell me. Tell me. At troubles I'm good."

I related to Miss. Kravitz everything that had happened between Jody and me. She was very consoling.

"Michael, Michael, discouraged you should not be. What was meant to be will be. But I will bet, 'Bells on Mine Bloomers,' that you two together again will be. Never did I tell you Michael, about when a young girl in Russia I was. In love I was with Ivanovitch, a young man of mine faith, he was not. A real love for each other it was. Not just a hot affair, it was. Secret meeting we had. Secret plans for some day when older, marry we would. But mine family found out and away they sent me to live with mine aunt and uncle. During the war his family hiding some Jewish people in their basement they were. The Germans found out and shot they were, his whole family but Ivanovitch taken away, he was. Never again did I see him. But never could I marry always thinking somewhere alive he was. And this thought in mine mind kept me alive."

"That's very sad and beautiful Miss Kravitz." She wiped her eyes with her apron.

"I haven't talked about it for years Michael. But the first time seeing you and your sandy blonde hair and blue eyes reminded me of mine own Ivanovitch, many years ago."

"Please don't cry Miss. Kravitz."

"You know Michael, I could maybe have a grandson like you today, if then different the world was."

"Let's pretend," I said as I put my arm around her shoulder and gave her an affectionate hug. "I'll call you Grandma Kravitz, how's that?"

"Happier I could not be. Thank you, Michael.

ELEVEN

Fighting The School Board

During the next week the Rowley School kept me too busy to think. I was notified that the meeting I had requested weeks ago, concerning this school, was scheduled to take place at the end of the week. Lucky for Bradshaw, Edgar had recovered from the beating in the school yard. As I walked into the office for the meeting Dr. Ling motioned me to join him. Tony was already there with Alan Katz, and other teachers from the school. Everyone was talking at once, and as I turned to see who else was there, from the different committees. Just then Jody entered the room. We stood for a moment without saying a word, and I could feel a tense strain as we gazed at each other. Her face clouded and she turned away and walked to the other end of the room. I wanted to rush after her but Mr. Hughes, the Assistant Superintendent of Schools stood up behind the long table and asked for everyone's attention.

"From what I understand there seems to be a feeling in this school that there are an undue amount of problems to handle. I'm sure you teachers realize that all schools have problems and that boys will be boys, restless, mischievous and full of energy.

Through the years we have seen some very successful students come out of the schools in Boston, some real winners! They have gone on to win scholarships, awards and become doctors and lawyers." I felt myself growing angrier by the second. Obviously, John Hughes would have continued relentlessly on every phase except the real problems facing this school. In a calm voice I interrupted.

"Mr. Hughes, I have requested this meeting not to talk about society's winners but to talk about society's losers. The kids that are suffering today from labels right here in our school! I question your use of the word 'mischievous'. Do you call students beating up their classmates because of their different religions, whamming clubs over their heads because they are black, mischievous? Mr. Hughes, we need this meeting here today in order to get some help because every day there are more young people getting more and more efficient in bigoted behavior. These students are acting like barbarians, and need to be stopped, now!" I said angrily. "I'm tired of standing by in this school and seeing young people abused because they are minorities. Something needs to be done about it!"

As I sat down Dr. Ling, our school psychologist stood up and continued. "Unfortunately we still find hatred and prejudice in today's world that was denounced thousands of years ago by Confucius, Hillel, Socrates and the Hebrew Prophets when they preached the Golden Rule which is also in Matthew 7:12, and only goes to show that human nature has not changed for

the better in forty thousand years."

For a moment a hush fell upon the room and then suddenly everyone started to speak at once.

"What's really sad," Tony De'Angelo's, powerful voice rose above the others, "is that it just isn't safe for these black kids to be bused into an all white neighborhood anymore than it is safe for whites to be bused into an all black neighborhood!"

"But you don't understand," Mr. Hughes started limply, "there is a theory around today that all children should be mixed with their fellow human beings, their fellow Americans, no matter what is the color of their skin."

Alan Katz rose up, "That's all very good in theory Mr. Hughes, but do you know the kind of name calling that goes on in this school? From early in the morning we hear these kids call each other; harp, wop, kike, polock, jungle bunnie, spick, kraut, chink, guinea, coon, Hebe, nigger, gook. nip, frog, wasp and I am sick of labels! These kids are intolerant, biased and have minds that are warped against people that are different than themselves!"

Mary Ann sauntered down the isle to the front of the room. She pulled down her sweater, adjusted her skirt and addressed the group. "Now, ah for one have never hated or been taught ta hate anyone in ma whole life, so ah can't possibly understand why these young people are carrying on this way. Ah have always believed in bringing love into the world an bringing people together. But, it is evident ta me that the only time the brown kids, the black kids, the white kids an the yellow kids would stick together is if suddenly, ah really strange looking green creature from another planet, invaded our school. An if this world don't stop hating so dam much, one day, someone is going ta press ah little red button, an then we will all be equal, invisible, an dead!"

As principal Bradshaw sat and coughed, and the shocked looks passed from teacher to teacher I said,

"It is true that the black children and others are being abused in school, but we teachers have to be alert enough to know when any trouble is brewing. There are sensitivity sessions for teachers which will help us learn to treat the symptoms of prejudice before it becomes a greater problem in our community. Unfortunately 766 cannot help these kids and unfortunately, a behavioral psychologist cannot help them, either. Today's bigoted children will be the parents of tomorrow who will pass on their unhealthy hate seeds into their future family system unless something is done about it. Those kids who attacked our other students said they were members of the Ku Klux Klan, which is a hate filled group that starts training their youth corps to use the twelve gauge shotgun and the M14 rifle at age ten. This is an organized group that is bent on violence against Catholics, blacks and Jews and is an ally of the Nazis. In fact, the Ku Klux Klan supported the German American Bund prior to World War Two. The Klan book publishing company promotes books like, 'The Hitler We Loved, 'White Power', the fraudulent 'Protocols of the Elders of Zion' and Hitler's, 'Mein Kampf,' to instill the seeds of Klan hate. Groups like these have been inculcated by the Russians for years to break up America, piece by piece. The Russians have planned that through our own internal turmoil we will eliminate peace in our land, and become receptive to their domination. Another 'Piece Plan' that the Russians are using is the one employed by Hitler in which he took over one country after another and eventually killed millions of civilians, of which only half were Jewish. If these hate-filled groups are allowed to continue because of our country's democratic belief in freedom of speech, then we must be vigilant and wise enough to see where it can lead.

The negative results of forced busing are overwhelming. According to surveys, assaults have grown while education has declined. There is no quality education at the end of the bus trip! Enforced busing has failed! What we need is freedom of choice! If parents and students decide they want to attend a predominantly minority school, predominantly white or racially balanced school, that should be their democratic right to choose! It is unfair to make innocent children suffer by not letting them attend schools within their own neighborhood, based only on the pigment of their skin!"

The assistant superintendent stood up.

"Friends, it's been two hours since this meeting started and we could talk for another two hours. Having been on the school scene for thirty-five years, I sympathize with everything you people are telling me, but it is out of my hands. Unfortunately, there is no special program in the city, state or country to rid us of prejudice, all we can hope to do is learn from past history in order to benefit from it. As far as the troublemakers in this school are concerned, I'm sure principal Bradshaw will take steps to see that this sort of thing does not happen again. I feel that high school age students can still change their way of thinking and learn about the dangers of prejudice, but the right kind of ideals and feelings for their fellow man begins at home, at a very, very young age."

Principal Bradshaw called for the close of the meeting and everyone got up to leave. Dr. Ling came over to me and talked about injustice. Tony knew I was very upset so he invited me over to his house. But all during the meeting I had felt Jody's eyes upon me so I waited until everyone left and she remained. Without saying anything I helped her on with her coat, and as her hair brushed against my face I bent down and kissed her.

"Michael, I missed you. I think we should talk."

"I've been hoping to hear those words for what has seemed like a million years, Jody." We rode around for a while and finally stopped at a little roadside restaurant. Sitting at the table, I took her hands in mine.

"You really had me worried should I keep worrying or can I stop?" I asked.

Jody's eyes lowered. "I feel very badly that I didn't give you a chance to explain before I rushed off to New York. I only know that the shock of your having been a priest, Michael, was too much for me to handle at that time. I had to leave to think things over."

"Jody, my feelings for you are everything I described when I wrote to you and more. No matter what you decide about us I'll always love you and I'll always feel that you loved me."

"You're right, Michael. I loved you and I still love you. I couldn't live without you for the rest of my life."

I squeezed her hands tightly.

"These past two weeks I spent thinking and talking to my Mother about us. She was very upset. I couldn't even discuss you with my Father. It's going to be difficult, if not impossible to persuade any of my family to accept our relationship."

"Just how much did you tell your Mother, Jody?"

"I explained how lonesome I was when I first came here and how you were one of the first friends I made. I told her that when I realized I was falling in love with you I stopped seeing you. Do you remember, Michael? That was when I came back from my holidays in New York."

"I remember."

"But then," she went on "as we worked together I saw what you were really like. I saw how you fought for what you believed in. You reminded me of my Father, Michael. That is when I really fell in love with you, and by then it was too late to turn back. I explained to Mother that the only thing that was keeping me from marrying you was our being of different religions. I said that I loved you very much but I didn't want to hurt them. I didn't tell Mother that you had been a priest for the same reasons you didn't tell me. Maybe some miracle will happen, Michael. Maybe if they meet you and get to know you they won't mind as much. I wish they heard you speak today at the meeting then they would have seen you for the person you really are and couldn't help but be proud."

We left the restaurant holding each other around the waist and walked through the gently falling snow to the car. Something about the soft white flakes on Jody's face made me plant a kiss on her lips.

"Michael, can't you wait until we get back to my apartment?" "Why do I have to wait until we get to your apartment?"

"So we can have coffee silly, what else?" And for the first time I noticed the twinkle and teasing look in her blue eyes as she smiled up at me.

TWELVE

Together

The inevitable day finally arrived, I was moving in with Jody. I kissed Miss Kravitz, my unofficially adopted grandmother, goodbye.

"Michael, I knew it vas going to be vun day I vould lose you." "I'm not going far Grandma Kravitz, and we will visit you often."

"I know, Michael. Just remember, ven it's married you get, mine house you can use. A hall it's not, but the rooms they are big."

"You'll be the first to know, Grandma, and thanks for everything." "Enjoy, Michael, enjoy and be happy." she said as I kissed her fondly on

the cheek.

"We're only around the corner so we will be seeing you very often. "And I'll have fresh challah vit holishkes for you which means mine

stuffed cabbage." she said as she stood at the door and waved goodbye.

Jody was at an art lecture in Boston when I moved my things into her apartment. We had become engaged, and I finally put that ring on her finger. As I finished hanging my clothes in the closet, she appeared, loaded down with fancy wrapped packages, which she dropped on the table.

"Open them up". She said.

"Hey, it's not my birthday, besides you said you were going to be at an important lecture all afternoon."

"I left early. I felt like buying you some things and wanted to help you unpack."

She gave me a big hug. "Go open the boxes, while I put the Chinese food out, and make tea."

The first box I opened held a maroon velvet bathrobe with my initials on the side in gold.

"Isn't it handsome, Michael? Try it on." It was a perfect fit, as were the sweaters and three shirts.

"Jody, you must have spent your whole paycheck on me."

"Now Michael, you never buy yourself very many clothes and besides," She called as she went in to take a shower, "I enjoy shopping for you!"

After what seemed like hours I knocked on the bathroom door. "If you're not out in another minute I'm coming in!"

I heard her give a light frivolous laugh, so I tried the door and finding it unlocked I went in. Quickly I undressed and stepped into the shower. The spray of warm water rained over us as I tightly clasped Jody's body to mine. Taking the soap I washed and decorated her magnificent breasts with suds. Her fingertips roamed lovingly over me while she lathered up my chest. As we laughed and stepped out of the shower I wrapped us both in one huge bath towel. Jody shivered in my arms as she whispered,

"Michael, kiss me the way you did on the sands of Rockport."

We looked into each others eyes as I held her tight and kissed her deeply. The bath towel dropped from us as I lifted her up, and carried her to our bed. Again she shivered. I tucked the blankets in around her and crawled in beside her. Under the blanket I ran my hand up and down her still damp body. "Michael, hold me, touch me all over. I like the feel of your hands on me."

She began to squirm with delight as my lips lightly brushed against her and tasted the sweet orange flavored bath oil on her nipples. She slid under me, and I found myself in a warm refuge as she folded her legs tightly around my hips and gasped, "Oh Michael!"

Seeing and feeling each movement of her incited me more, and as she increased her rhythm it became harder and harder to hold back.

"Does it feel good Jody?"

"Michael the way you make me feel is wonderful." She uncontrollably dug her fingernails into my shoulders and at the same moment a torrent burst inside me. We had reached the apex together. Gently I withdrew from my sanctuary and lay down beside her relaxed and content.

"Jody, Jody Ich liebe du."

"Ich liebe du Michael". (I love you)

I looked at her well endowed breasts. "I see our kids won't need to be bottle fed."

"We're not quite ready for babies Michael."

"Do you want children Jody?"

"Of course silly, children, dogs, cats, house, picket fence, the works! I want to be able to give my kids all the things I never had. What about you Michael? What kind of a childhood did you have?"

"Well, being an only child, like you, I always had a lot of love and attention not only from my folks, but also from my Grandfather who always lived with us. He taught me many things and took me everywhere. We always had animals around the house and I really enjoyed my years at home."

"What about your school days?" "I went to private schools." "And summers?"

"Summers I went to camp except when my folks took me traveling with them."

"Traveling?"

"Yes, we traveled to different countries. We went to Japan, Hawaii, parts of the United States and South America a few times. My Mother has relatives there."

"We really do come from completely different backgrounds." I cupped Jody's face in the palm of my hand, lifting it up.

"I think we are enough alike to be happy together. No life is without obstacles, and real love can surmount almost any pressures if two people want to work at it together."

"Michael you always know what to say and you speak so eloquently. One day you should put your thoughts down on paper. It would make a fascinating book."

"I started a book four years ago, so you can expect to hear me typing late at night."

"What's it about?"

"It's a history book about the roots of religion." "I hope I hear you typing often Michael."

We finally went into the kitchen and reheated the Chinese food. "Today is a celebration. It is our first, 'At Home Together Meal," Jody

remarked as she put the candles on the table, lit them, and shut the lights. "This is perfect," she said. "Let's enjoy it now while we can because after

we eat I'm calling my family to tell them our wedding plans."

We finished dinner, washed the dishes and Jody sat down to put in a very nervous phone call to New York. As she dialed the number she asked me to sit next to her, while she talked.

"Hello Mother, how are you? I'm fine. How's Dad? How much did you tell him? You mean he just walked out? How long was he gone? Has he still got a fever? Dr. Feingersh. Tell him I still love him. Mother I know but I can't change my mind. No ones making up my mind for me Mother. I have thought it all out. I'm the same girl I use to be, I'm just older. All right then, I don't want to change my mind! But I love him Ma. I've gone out with others. I'm going to be twenty-five Mother. Can I speak to Dad? I don't want to upset him. Mother, I love you and Dad but I love Michael, too. Mother, we set a wedding date. Nothing can change my mind. It's definite! It's the twenty-fifth of June on a Sunday. Hello, Hello Mother? Won't you even meet him? You would like him once you got to know him. I told you about his family. His father works for the United States government. He's the head of immigration. They were in the resistance. No, I haven't met them yet. Tell Papa I love him and to please get well. All right Mama." Jody hung up the phone.

"What's the matter with your Father?"

"Ma told him about us after I left there the other day and he was so upset that he ran out of the house and walked for hours in the blizzard. Now, he's sick with a bad cold."

Just then the phone rang and Jody answered.

"Hello I'm sorry you're sick pa. Yes, I made up my mind. He's not like that! You would like him if you met him! Yes, please Papa, I know what they did to your arm, but Michael wasn't even born then! His folks sound like they are wonderful people. You have to come to my wedding because I love you. Please Pa, don't say that! Hello? Hello?" Jody put the receiver back.

"He hung up on me." Jody wiped her tearing eyes and I hugged her to me and stroked her head.

"Oh Michael, what can we do to make him understand?"

"We may not be able to do anything, liebchen. Now we will wait and see what my folks have to say. I wrote them about us last night."

"They probably will feel the same way as my family does!"

"No. I don't think so. My Mother and Father have nothing against Jewish people. In fact, they have Jewish friends in many places and my father has Jewish business acquaintances. Mother may even have a family party to meet you."

"Who would be there Michael?"

"It wouldn't be a large party only my Mother, Father and possibly his brother Ludwig, and my Grandfather, who lives with my folks. Wait till you see the paintings my Grandfather does. You two will have a lot to talk about, you'll like him."

It was a week later when a surprise phone call came in from Mrs. Loeb. Jody looked at me quizzically as I handed her the phone.

Hello Ma, Yes, we can be there next weekend. Ma, you are an angel! Saturday about twelve noon, we'll drive up." Jody looked at me questioningly, and I nodded yes.

"Will Dad be there? Please try to have him there. Thank you, Ma. I love you!" Jody hung up the phone, all smiles this time. "Mike, Mother wants to meet you.

She hasn't told Father yet about our coming but she feels that since we set the date for the wedding, we should all meet. Maybe my Aunt Frieda will be there. Our families are very close. She has treated me like a daughter ever since I can remember."

"I hope things work out Jody. I've seen people go through this before, and sometimes they won't even talk to each other. Sometimes they all meet for the first time at the wedding. You may as well be prepared for anything." "Michael, as hostile as my Father appears to be concerning our marriage,

I think he loves me enough to accept the situation, now that we have made definite plans. Before, he probably figured we might still change our minds. I do have to wait to tell my family about your being a former priest. I wish I didn't have to make them so unhappy." she said sadly. "If I find everything goes well this weekend I will tell my Mother all about you and then later she can tell my Father, when she thinks it's wise, like after he has a good meal."

THIRTEEN

Judith's Family

Saturday morning finally arrived. I found Jody already dressed and in the kitchen making breakfast. She was always fast and efficient but this morning I could feel her excitement penetrate the very air. As she smiled she pulled out the chair for me and then she announced, "Two sunny side days, coming up, with toast on the side, right Mike?"

"I hope so Jody."

After breakfast we took our overnight suitcases and proceeded on to New York. The four and a half hour drive was pleasant with Jody snuggled beside me in the car, happy and hopeful that everything was going to work out well. On reaching New York Jody directed me to the Pelham Bay Area of the Bronx where her folks had their apartment. We rode past kids playing on the congested street and parked in front of a Jewish butcher shop.

Jody pointed out the six story tenement building in which her Mother and Father lived. We walked up the two flights of stairs and Jody knocked on the door.

"Hello, anyone home?" She called. A pleasant faced woman opened the door, smiled happily at Jody and kissed her affectionately. Jody introduced me to her Mother, who was a very pretty woman around fifty with dark hair and warm brown eyes with a tendency toward middle aged plumpness. But she looked nothing like Jody. She shook my hand nervously as she smiled and said, "Welcome children, come into the living room and join us." We followed her into the book lined room which was simply but comfortably furnished with an old upright piano in the corner. Over on the couch Mrs. Loeb's sister,

Frieda, thin, blonde and well dressed sat next to her husband Abe, who was of medium build and had a gentle, smiling face. Their son, Sherman sat next to them. They kissed and hugged Jody jubilantly and greeted me in a friendly but cool manner. From their expressions I felt I was being studied, part by part, disassembled, and then reassembled for further examination, especially by eight year old Sherman. Aunt Frieda monopolized Jody for the first half hour and then apologized by saying,

"Judith Is like my own daughter, we have been very close and I've missed her."

"Where is Dad?" Jody asked her Mother.

"He went to the grocery store. He should be back any minute."

Little Sherman was sitting and staring at me. Slowly he got up and started circling around me as he looked me over from top to bottom.

Then suddenly in a loud voice he questioned, "Are you a Nazi?"

"Sherman!" His mother yelled, "You don't talk like that!"

Obviously, I thought to myself, someone had been doing a lot of talking in front of this child.

"But Mama," he yelled, "you said his family could have been Nazis!" "Quiet Sherman, you didn't understand what we said. Go sit by the

window and watch television."

I took the boy's hand. "Sherman," I said, "not everyone in Germany was a Nazi and besides, I was born in this country. I'm an American just like you. So how about our being friends?"

There was silence, then, "I don't know if I like you yet. Are you going to marry my cousin Judith?"

"I plan to marry your cousin. Will you come to the wedding?"

"I'll come to the wedding if my mother lets me." He looked me up and down again.

"Did you have a Bar Mitzvah? He asked.

"No, but I hope you will invite me to your Bar Mitzvah one day." As the child ran off into the other room Uncle Abe remarked,

"Don't mind Sherman. Come, have a drink with us. I joined them with a drink while they made small talk which was meant to put me at ease, but was filled with inquisitive overtones.

"I understand your family lives in Washington." Abe remarked. "Just outside in Chevy Chase." I answered.

"Oh, that's a very, very nice section."

"My husband has business acquaintances that live out there." Frieda said. "Is your Father working for the government a long time Michael?" Abe

asked. "About ten years." I answered

Abe offered me a cigar but I explained I was a pipe smoker. Just as I started filling my pipe Abe commented,

"I hear your Father has a very important position, a very responsible position."

"Yes, he's the head of immigration."

"Didn't you ever want to go into government work Michael? Were you always a teacher?" Frieda asked.

"Well not always". I answered between puffs on my pipe.

I could feel the next question coming just as Jody walked in with a tray of hors d'oeuvres.

"What did you do before you decided to teach?" Frieda continued. "Michael not only teaches but he writes." Jody offered.

"Oh, you are a writer!' Jody's Mother said, as she came into the room. "How nice." her aunt commented, "Have you published anything?" "Not yet but maybe one day," I replied.

"I wish your Father could hear this. I don't know what is keeping him.

We'll wait a few more minutes if he's not back we will sit down and eat." "But Ma, he only went down the street, didn't he?"

"Don't ask so many questions, Judith, just pass around some hors d'oeuvres to your friend Michael. He looks hungry."

I took a few hors d'oeuvre and walked over to the shelves filled with books and noticed almost everyone was about music. Jody had told me about her mother giving piano lessons in their home and I remarked to Mrs. Loeb that I would enjoy hearing her play.

"I'm really not that talented at playing the piano Michael. I'm better   at teaching. It's my husband who had the talent in music. He was a child prodigy. In fact at the age of six he gave his first piano concert in Berlin. He would have had a very successful career if things had been different. Instead," she said with a shrug, "he rents musical instruments from our home."

It was now seven o'clock and there was no sign of Jody's Father. I could see everyone was very upset. Her mother kept very busy running nervously between the kitchen and the living room where she had put up an extension table.

Back and forth she went glancing out of the window at every opportunity. While Abe was watching television with Sherman and Frieda was busy setting up the dinner table Jody went in to her mother in the kitchen. I couldn't help but overhear them talking since my chair was next to the kitchen door.

"Where Is Father? I didn't think he would do this to me. We wouldn't have come if I knew."

"Please Judith, your Father may walk in yet. You know how unpredictable he is.

He's a very emotional man who has gone through too much for any one person and now, again he suffers. Why couldn't you have wanted to marry someone like Bernie Goldberg who is a nice Jewish boy, a professional man, a father that's a doctor and good friends of ours?"

"Don't you like Michael, at all Mother?"

"He seems like a mensch. (decent sort) It's just too bad he isn't a Jewish mensch!"

"Mother, Michael may not be Jewish but he is a very wonderful human being, and I love him! He knows all about the Jewish religion and understands and can explain the Bible better than most people. He has told me things about religion that very few people know. Mother, Michael has had more experience than being just an ancient history teacher. You might say he is really a scholar, who is very knowledgeable in theology."

"Judith, I know you very well, in fact, no one knows you any better than your own Mother. And right now I am getting a feeling in the pit of my stomach that is not from the stuffed mushrooms we had for appetizers!"

"Mother, don't get upset."

"Who is upset? My one and only educated, beautiful, talented daughter is going to marry out of our Jewish faith. Who is upset? Judith, let's get to the point. What are you leading up to? How come your friend, Michael, is so knowledgeable about religion?

"Mother how upset would you become if you learned Michael had once been in the clergy?"

"Now I suppose you are going to tell me he was a Catholic Rabbi? I'm getting your message Judith. Your young man was a Priest!"

"But he gave it up Mother! He gave it up before he met me!"

"I see Judith, now it's all out in the open. Now let's stop before I drop everything and completely collapse from you! I hope your Father doesn't come in tonight. I don't think I can stand much more!"

There was silence in the kitchen until a few minutes later when Frieda went in to help them bring out the food. We all sat around the table eating except Uncle Abe and Jody's Father who had not showed up.

"What's the matter Abe?" Jody Mother asked, "You've hardly filled your plate. Isn't my dinner tempting you tonight?"

"You know Fanny, I eat very carefully lately. I watch my health foods and my diet. I work out at the gym twice a week. I get a good rub-down at the massage parlor next door to my garment business and"

"That's the place where the girls rub you and Ma don't want you to go there anymore, Dad!" Sherman brightly remarked as he pulled the wish bone apart.

"Your Mother doesn't care where I go as long as I give her money so she can visit Bloomingdales everyday. Then she's happy! In fact when I die I am going to have my body cremated and the ashes dropped over Bloomies, that way I'll know my wife will visit me everyday."

"That's not very nice to say Abe. You make it sound like all I do is shop." "Why, do you do something else? You and all your girlfriends keep

the stores in business. Michael, did you ever stop to think what wonderful leaders our women of today are? They are like generals. Every time I go into a department store I hear them yelling their battle cry, 'charge!'"

I tried to stifle a laugh as Uncle Abe continued.

"Michael I give my wife a full time maid, a cleaning woman for the heavy work, so the full time maid doesn't get tired and quit, nurse for Sherman, a beautiful new car every year, gorgeous home in Kings Grant Long Island, and all she does is bring me home bargains and tell me how much money she saves me!"

"Abe, that is quite enough!" Frieda sounded disturbed. Jody took the conversation in hand,

"We were going to wait until Father came in to tell everyone about our wedding plans but I guess it's no secret. Michael and I are getting married in June." Judith put her hand in mine,

"Mazel tov, which means, 'may your planet be good to you.' "Uncle Abe said.

"Congratulations." Frieda said." And who is going to perform the ceremony?"

"We're not quite sure yet." Jody answered. Uncle Abe suggested,

"Why don't you get married In New York? We certainly have beautiful weddings here! Just last Saturday night we went to a wedding with five hundred people. We didn't finish eating until four o'clock Sunday morning. Then we went to the home of the brides parents in Scarsdale where she had a catered brunch."

"We are having a very simple wedding and we hope everyone in the family will come," Jody announced looking at her mother.

"I would like to offer our home for the wedding", Aunt Frieda volunteered. "And in June you could even have it out in the garden by the swimming

pool." Abe chimed in.

We thanked them for their offer, saying we would keep it in mind. "Sherman, you're eating like a bird!" Frieda reprimanded him. "Don't

you know people are starving all over the world?"

"Yes, Mother, that's what you've been telling me for eight years now!"

We finished dessert and got up from the table. Mr. Loeb still hadn't come in and Jody's mother looked worried. We talked until about nine-thirty when Sherman became restless and Frieda and Abe decided to leave. They said good- bye and firmly pushed Sherman out the door. Just at that moment I saw a tall heavy set man walking up the stairs. One look at his finely molded features, high forehead and deep, large set blue eyes identified him at once as Jody's Father. His face was set in a determined frown as he pushed his way up the stairs past Sherman. Frieda gave him a little hug, and whispered in his ear as she went down the stairs, while Abe slapped him affectionately on the shoulder.

Immediately Jody went over and kissed him on the cheek as he glanced at me out of the corner of his eye.

"Father, we missed you at dinner. I'd like you to meet Michael Ulricke.

Michael, my Father."

Automatically I extended my hand to Mr. Loeb but quickly retracted it, realizing my mistake. He responded with a cold piercing look which communicated to me at once that he regarded me with obvious disdain. Through tight set lips be murmured,

"Vit a stump you can't shake hands Mr.Ulricke, that vas my gift from the Nazis!" I felt annoyed at myself that I had made such a faux pas and wondered if I would ever be able to win over this openly hostile man. Jody's Mother interrupted us,

"Your dinners warm and waiting for you Max."

"I already ate downtown. I'm tired. I'm going to bed."

"But Father, we haven't spent any time with you. We haven't had a chance to talk,"

"You want to talk? Vat is there to talk about?" He swung his left hand in the air as if to brush aside any further communication,

"Here Max," Mrs. Loeb said, "have a cup of tea with apple strudel before you go to sleep." He sat down looking very worn and unhappy. I thought to myself how obviously he reflected the suffering of so many people. We all sat quietly as Mr. Loeb drank his tea.

After a few minutes Jody's mother broke the silence.

"You know Max, Judith's friend Michael is writing a book."

"So vat's new? Who isn't writing a book? Someday even I vill write a story.

A story about how my family vas the victims of hate! How they ver tortured and their bodies torn apart!"

"Max, don't get so excited, remember your blood pressure.

"Father, Michael's book is called, 'Religions of the Past.' Mr. Loeb looked up and I noticed a flicker of interest in his angry face.

"I had done a lot of historical research during my college days which made me decide to write a book starting with the religion of the stone age tribes." I said.

"That vas when their saviors gave the vorld a mental indigestion! You should write a book Mr. Ulricke, vich tells the vorld that because the prophet Isaiah, has been misinterpreted the world has been torn apart! You should write that Isaiah did not vant another resurrected savior up high. I know my bible very vell, Mr. Ulricke, and it says in Isaiah 26:14. 'They are dead, they shall not live; they are deceased, they shall not rise.' Isaiah vanted a human son of man! He wanted a leader on earth who vould be the Messiah that vould change the swords to ploughshares and bring peace! Mr. Ulricke, I say the earth is going to have 'shalom' (peace) very soon. The tulips' vill come up in the springtime. The grains vill rise from the fields, but there vill be no one around to enjoy it. Each time it started vit the Jews, but this time vit neutron rays, everyone goes!"

Jody's Mother tried to calm down her husband but he only continued in a louder voice,

"You should write about the lies in the book called, The Protocols of The Elders of Zion', concerning the sect of Essene Jews. Somevun should explain how the Essene Jews sent missionaries out to preach peace and love. How these people did not vant to rule the world but to escape from its vicious conditions. You should write how the unarmed Essene Jews never vanted to create a military empire of an Alexander, a Caesar or a Napoleon or a Hitler! Their hope vas for an earthly teacher to create a peace on earth, but instead it developed into a mystical dream of an earthly Messiah."

In a voice again filled with emotion Mr. Loeb asked,

"Did you know the Dead Sea Scrolls prove that vay back, vun hundred and sixty five years before your Paul vas born, the Essene Jews ver already vaiting for vun of their holy men to return to the earth from the underworld? Vay back then it vas written in the scrolls that the Essene Jews ver vaiting for this holy man who had been flayed and crucified and vould now be put back together again. Humpty Dumpty couldn't be put back together again but the Essenes ver vaiting for this resurrected person to come back to earth! Ve did not know this until the Dead Sea Scrolls ver found because even the Essene Jews ver viped out.'

Mr. Loeb looked at me as he finished his tea, "Tell me Mr. Ulricke, vot made you decide to write a book about religion? Was it my daughter?"

"No, I thought of this long before Judith."

"Ulricke, you say your name is Ulricke? A Nazi doctor vas at one of the concentration camps by that name."

"I am sure he was not related to my family, Mr. Loeb."

"Father, Michael's grandparents were in the Resistance to the Nazis! They never hurt a Jew, if anything they helped them and hid them from the Nazis. Isn't that right Michael?"

"Yes, they were very instrumental in getting Jewish people over the border to Switzerland. My family, my Grandfather especially told me about this many times as I was growing up."

"Maybe so Mr. Ulricke, but I cannot forgive and I cannot forget the anti-semitism which helped Hitler and his Nazis grow powerful and destroy my people. And you Mr. Ulricke," he said in a raised voice as he shook his one hand and pointed his finger at me, "Ven you get angry vit my Judith vill you suddenly see her only as another Jew?"

"Mr. Loeb," I said in a raised voice, "you forget that millions of Christians were killed because of Hitler and his Nazi gang!"

"Father, Michael and I love each other. Has the war destroyed your seeing things clearly? Are you so blind that you only see with hate?"

"I see only that ve Jews have died out from two things vun is hate and the other is love!" I noticed that his eye started to twitch nervously.

"Tell me Mr. Ulricke, vhy is it you feel you vant to marry a Jewish girl?" "I'm not marrying Judith because she is Jewish, French, German or Spanish, black or white. I love her and she loves me. That is why we are

getting married."

"You are getting married you say? Vell if my daughter ever marries out of her faith, to me she vould be, like dead!" With this remark her Father abruptly rose from his chair, swung his hand and knocked over the lamp as he ran from the room yelling,

"You throw your family avay, all for a tumble in the bed sheets!"

Jody was sitting and crying at the table as her Mother said with a choked voice,

"I'm sorry children, but Judith, you knew, a long time ago, what your Father's feelings were towards a marriage outside our faith!

"I thought he would act differently after he met Michael and realized we were serious about getting married."

"Michael there is nothing I can say," Mrs. Loeb explained, "you seem like a nice clean cut young man but Judith's Father is not going to relent! He feels nothing has changed since World War II and that anti-Semitism is still here and has led to Hitler and all our suffering. Even now, after all these years, your Father still has nightmares about his childhood. He saw his little six year old sister shot and his three month old baby brother grabbed at the ankle by a Nazi soldier who swung him around and smashed his head against the sink in their house. Max was only ten at the time this happened and he remembers it like yesterday. He saw his mother raped by a German officer and his father dragged away and shot when he tried to protect her. He never saw them again. These are his last impressions of his loved ones. I'm sorry children", she cried and wiped her tears. "I certainly didn't want you to have such an unpleasant time here tonight."

"You did your best Mother," Jody said as she hugged her. "We better leave.

I don't want to be here if Father comes in again."

"But it's so late for you children to travel. I had hoped you both would stay over tonight."

"It's best we leave Mrs. Loeb," I said and I kissed her on the cheek.

Judith embraced her Mother and as they clung together the tears streamed down their faces. We promised her Mother we would let her know the plans we made and walked out the door and down the stairs to the car, sad and disheartened. On the drive home we fell into a deep silence, each thinking our own thoughts. It started to rain and Jody moved closer to me, her head leaning against my arm.

"Mike", she started, "whatever feelings you got tonight about my Father, please try and understand that he's not really what he seemed. It's not a question of his being 'intolerant' or his being 'clannish'. He is trying, in the only way he knows, to keep his family from being assimilated or swallowed up by people who he feels have made the Jew suffer through the centuries. He doesn't see you as an individual. He is afraid to let himself."

"Don't try to apologize for your Father, Jody. It's the world that really owes him an apology. I felt very bad when I heard what he had gone through." Jody wrapped her hand around my elbow.

"I really love them so much, Michael, and I hate making them unhappy."

A few minutes later I looked down to see she had fallen asleep and I drove on to Boston.

FOURTEEN

The Belly Dance

Monday, as I left my homeroom deep in thought about our visit with Jody's family, Mary Ann unexpectedly approached me. "Michael, why do ya wear such a frown on ya handsome face? Did ya have a fight with Bradshaw?" she asked as she walked beside me towards the teacher's room. "Bradshaw is retiring this year, why don't ya try ta get his job? With your background I'm sure ya could get it. Besides, with ya getting married an Jody wanting a house an kids an all, you'll need a lot more money than ya getting ta make her happy! Ya going ta have ta learn how ta support a Jap, that's short fa, Jewish American Princess."

"Mary Ann, Jody is far from spoiled. I hope someday I will be able to spoil her. She and her family both deserve it. Besides, I'm getting fed up with your picking on her!"

"But honey, I'm not! It's just that ah can't see the two of ya married. Ya both are so different. You're a very sexy man, Michael, and ya know what they say about 'her kind,'"

"No. I don't know what they say about ' her kind' as you put it, and I don't want to know!"

"They say," her voice rolled on," 'her kind' gives a guy plenty ah bait, an after they reel 'em in, they just lay there like cold fish! And ah can't see ya married to ah flounder!"

"Is that another made up joke about 'her kind', Mary Ann?" I asked angrily, as I walked into the teacher's lounge for a cup of coffee.

"Ah don't want ya ta think ah have anything against Jody", she continued, "in fact, Charles an I would like ta have ya both ta dinner at 'our apartment' next Saturday night."

I was surprised to hear she and Charles were living together. I hadn't pegged him to be such a fast worker. Although Jody and I both liked Charles, we had been embarrassed more than once by Mary Ann's extreme personality and had tried to keep our distance, but when he telephoned and insisted we come over we found it hard to say no.

Saturday night, seven p.m. sharp, we rang their doorbell. Charles opened the door with Mary Ann clinging to him, as if they were all part of the same body. They greeted us with kisses as they took our coats and the bottle of wine we had brought.

"How would ya all like ta see our apartment?" Mary Ann asked as Charles put his arm around her and she kissed him on the cheek.

"Ma big boy here is so affectionate he won't let me alone for a moment. Do ya notice how perfect Charles's furniture fits in ma apartment? In fact, everything Charles has fits in perfect." she laughed.

"Baby doll is such a joker, "Charles commented. "Tell me what will you have to drink? We have a bar with just about anything you can ask for. How about starting the evening with a champagne toast?" As he poured the champagne I noticed a change had come over Charles, other than his toupee. He seemed much happier and laughed more than during the years I had known him as a priest.

"Let's make a toast", Charles said. "To Adam's sons who've gone astray and to all Eve's daughters who like to play. Remember that one from the Parish Mike?"

Before I could speak Mary Ann suggested, "How about ya all trying ma appetizers? Charles has been dying for these succulent raw oysters but ah wouldn't let him try any till ya all came."

"They look interesting, Mary Ann, Jody said as she picked one up and dropped it into my mouth.

"Wait until ah seduce ya palate with the rest ah ma food. Mary Ann went on.

Ah have been cooking from an Aphrodisiac cookbook an Charles just loves it! You two will never forget that ya came ta dinner at our place an tried ma special culinary seductions. Of course science is only aware ah two truly sexually stimulating foods, that's Spanish Fly and Yohimbine but ya know, the plain little ole sweet potato has an awful lot ah hormones of her own!"

"Did you know," Charles asked, "there was once an Arabian Sheik, who had the disease Satyriasis, who satisfied a harem of one hundred concubines in a week? What a disease! But believe me Mary Ann's food is almost as good as getting Satyriasis!" He smiled."

"An eating it is as good as being seduced. Isn't that right Charles?" Mary Ann asked.

"It is almost, almost like it, sweetheart.

"Ah have the menu right here in ma hand. Would ya all like ta hear it?" "I feel like we're at a restaurant, what's on the menu?" Jody asked. "Thank ya darling. Well, we will start with ah Sensuous Salad. Then

ah will serve ya Fervor Fruits, made with ah wee bit ah Cointreau liqueur, ta wet ya appetite. The main course is Fondue Fallatio, covered with flaming brandy."

Jody and I looked at each other questioningly.

"Ma Piece de Resistance is called Custard Climax" Jody said.

"It sounds like you're preparing us for an orgy." Jody told Mary Ann," but we'll try anything once, right Michael?"

"Savoir manger savoir vivre". (To know how to eat is to know how to live.) I said as I rolled my eyes at Jody, and wondered what was in store for us. "Don't worry, after ya taste it I'll bet ya are going ta want to borrow ma cookbook Jody, an award me the 'Cordon Bleu!'

Now if you will all sit down we can partake of ma Aphrodisiac Foods." "I think that name stems from the Greek Goddess Aphrodite, who was

the Goddess of Love and Beauty."

"That is right Jody, and it is so good to have Mary Ann an ardent food lover." Charles informed us. "If more people were like her there would be less sex therapy necessary in the world." After dinner, as I smoked my pipe, I looked over the books in the apartment.

"These are all Charles books," Mary Ann told me. "Ah appreciate his great mind." she said as she draped herself over him on the couch and gave him a long loving kiss.

Charles then raised his glass and drank another toast to his Mary Ann.

As she sat on his lap he continued.

"Mary Ann has given me a new lease on life. She has taught me to be a free thinking and feeling man. She has freed me sexually from my inhibited, old fashioned, restrained ways of yesterday." Charles took another drink. "There is nothing like being in love with a free thinking woman to realize what a deprived man one used to be. Isn't that right Mike?"

"Free thinking, Charles, I'm all for it."

"Come on everyone," Charles said, "let's all drink to the free thinkers of the world!" Again we drank a toast. We continued toasting throughout the evening. The girls were chatting in the kitchen but Charles, being rather tipsy only wanted to talk about his wonderful Mary Ann.

"We have been fused into one! Mike, she is unbelievable. You can't imagine what we have together. I've lost fifteen pounds since I've been with her.

I lost it in bed making love. We make love for hours at a time, and there's no exercise in the world like it. It beats tennis! I've had lots of girls before I became a priest and after I gave it up but Mary Ann is unusual. She has a thing!"

"Now Charles, we've been drinking, and you've had a little too much.

Maybe you shouldn't tell me all this."

"You won't remember it tomorrow anyway Mike. It is fantastic. Our sex is like the music from a Stradivarius! Charles bent down and whispered in my ear. "Did you ever hear of a girl that was built, 'horizontal?"

"You mean to say. "Yes, down there."

"No. I don't think I have. There's no such thing."

"Oh yes there is. I know because Mary Ann is built, 'horizontal', and it's out of this world!"

I thought to myself about the night she had come to my apartment. She had been a terrific lay and at the time I didn't question why and I didn't wonder how. I only knew it had been impossible to stop.

"But we are more than just sexually attracted to one another," Charles continued. "I respect Mary Ann for her honesty. She isn't one who believes in putting fig leaves on Greek statues! She has told me of her unhappy exploits and described her debaucheries. She has been very unlucky in her marriages."

"Mary Ann's been married?"

"Oh yes Michael, three times, but all her marriages were very short lived.

Each husband left her." "They left her?"

"Yes, they left her unwillingly. They all died. I looked at Charles and wondered just what significance he put on this.

"But Mary Ann keeps herself very busy so she doesn't think of her unhappy past. She is even going to night school now."

"What is she studying there?"

"She is studying dancing. She is the most exotic belly dancer! She can give life to a stone with her dancing." Just then the girls came into the living room.

"How about doing some dancing for us honey?" Charles asked.

"Ah would be delighted, just wait two seconds an I'll get into ma costume." Mary Ann disappeared and Charles changed the record on his stereo to a seductive beat, and announced, "You're in for a treat!" Jody and I sat holding hands and drinking our sherry as Mary Ann sauntered out of the bedroom. Her garments were as sheer as rose petals. A 'G String' covered her loins giving a southern exposure while 'pasties' clung to her breasts leaving nothing to the imagination. She stood in front of us, her eyes downcast, her hands folded. She radiated sex as she began undulating with the heavy beat of the music.

She could provoke any man with her body motions and Jody looked at me as I held her close. Charles stared with entranced eyes as Mary Ann submitted to the pulsating rhythmical song. The music throbbed while she danced and made exciting gestures with her arms and legs. She increased her movements in an enticing manner as the tempo grew faster and faster. She spread her legs apart and gyrated tauntingly. One really needed to use strategy to retain one's semen! Charles watched her, his hungry eyes fascinated.

His passion for her was obviously visible, as her body danced erotically in front of him.

She revealed her shapely thighs to goggle eyed Charles. The music stopped and Mary Ann ended her dance with legs spread apart in front of the face of Charles, who leaped to his feet, staggering as he did so and stumbled into the arms of half naked Mary Ann. I clapped loudly, breaking the lustful atmosphere for Charles, and reminding him that we were still there.

"What do you think of my girl, isn't she terrific?" He asked. "Jody, why don't you take lessons with Mary Ann?" Charles continued, "Just think what it would do for Michael, if you danced like that."

"She excites me enough already Charles."

"Maybe I should take lessons Michael, we may enjoy it." We decided to leave the two sex pots alone, said our-farewells and left. On the ride home Jody commented on how Mary Ann's dancing affected Charles and said,

"Confess Michael, wouldn't you like me to be able to dance like that?" "You already do Jody, and we're going home now to dance just like she

did but together and lying down."

As soon as we entered our apartment Jody walked over to the stereo and put on a record with an enticing beat. She danced around the room trying to imitate the erotic dance of Mary Ann. My appetite had already been whetted so as Jody danced in front of me I began taking off her clothes one by one, until she stood before me completely naked.

Jody submitted herself to my inspection but held me at arms length. My eyes caressed her voluptuous breasts, her flat stomach, her round full hips, and her pudendum. Her exquisite, provocative body was the sublime representation of perfection. To see it was to love it. No man could look at it without instant desire.

"I will never let you dance before any other man but me!" I told her filled with emotion. I cupped her breasts with my hands and said "Those little 'Pasties' would never stay on you."

"They stay on Mary Ann." Jody insisted.

"That's because she has little violets and yours are big, beautiful Chrysanthemums!" I could feel her fast heartbeat as I tipped her face up and kissed it. We got into bed, and showing no partiality, I kissed her breasts one by one. I looked up at her face, her eyes were closed, her lips parted. Frantic, urgent sensations rushed from my stomach, down to my loins. Her legs came up around me as I penetrated inside her. With each creak of the bed she moaned with delight as our desires were fulfilled.

FIFTEEN

The Winter Solstice

It was during my coffee break when I passed the music room that I heard the angry voices of Mary Ann and Jody. I walked in and saw Principal Bradshaw vainly trying to stop their fight.

"I don't know why you have to interfere with Mary Ann!" Bradshaw said indignantly to Jody. She has directed our Christmas, Chanukah program for the last five years and no one has complained. In fact, parents who have seen it have complimented us on this wonderful interfaith program! You're a new teacher here. You've never taught in any other school before. What gives you the right to criticize what we are doing for our holiday program?"

Jody looked exasperated and answered, "This is not an interfaith program that I am doing the artwork for because there are children in this school who are of the Buddhist and Muslim faiths that are not represented at all and Chanukah is not being told correctly! It has been reduced to a holiday of latkes (pancakes) and the miracle of oil burning for eight days!" As Jody stood talking in a raised voice which I had never heard before, Mary Ann ran over to me and tugged at my sleeve. "Mike, your girlfriend is making an awful row about nothing! Will you please get her out of here?"

I walked over to Principal Bradshaw who stared at me with a grim look on his face. "What are you doing here?" He questioned me sharply.

"I couldn't help overhearing your discussion."

"And you haven't seen our interfaith program so don't start telling me your version of upholding the Constitution of the United States, and separation of church and state!" Bradshaw barked at me.

"Well, if you teach the history of religions without any devotional music or prayers, which really are proselytizing, then it could be acceptable." I said. "Listen Michael, I know you were once a priest but your friend here," he said as he pointed to Jody, "wants to change the whole aspect of Chanukah,

as we know it, and as we have been presenting it for years."

"But what they are doing is wrong." Jody persisted. "They don't want to make a change and they are teaching history incorrectly. You are an ancient history teacher Michael. Tell them the true story of Chanukah."

"Go ahead, Mike," Mary Ann encouraged. "Ma mind is open."

"Well, in 529 B.C.E. the Hebrew people freed themselves from their pagan gods.

That is when Judaism was born. But then Antiochus IV insisted that all Jews be converted to the Greek religion and worship their gods or be tortured and killed.

"This was the first religious holocaust!" Jody added as Michael continued. "But a young Jew called, Judas Maccabeus, came along with his men who fought against Antiochus with the help of Gentiles who smuggled arms to Judas. This was the first holy war and it lasted for three years. Judas defeated the pagan soldiers, went back to the Jewish temple and rededicated it to the unborn God Jehovah. Then with one days supply of sacred oil they lit the eternal light that miraculously burned for eight days.

Judas was enshrined from then on for his victory over paganism by the holiday of Chanukah."

"That was so interesting, Michael. Ya make it so easy ta understand." Mary Ann said as she gave Michael a flirtatious smile.

"Now you know why I wanted him as our history teacher." Principal Bradshaw announced as the bell rang and everyone went to their next class.

SIXTEEN

Michael's Family

When I called my parents and told them about our marriage plans they seemed surprised and pleased. They wanted to meet Jody before the wedding, so I made arrangements for us to go there the following month during our spring vacation.

Mother told me Grandfather was visiting friends in South America but would be back in time to see us. She made a point of my not mentioning Jody's religion in front of Grandfather. She said she felt it might prove embarrassing. I couldn't understand this because I had grown up hearing stories about how he had saved many Jewish lives during World War Two. I asked mother what had changed his feelings and she told me about some of his new friends who had unfortunately altered his thinking. When I expressed my disgust for this attitude and suggested it might be better that we did not come, she pleaded with me to forgive Grandfather for his crazy ideas because of his old age. Finally, I agreed we would come for a very short visit. At that time, I was still completely unaware of the truth concerning my family.

The day in April finally arrived when a little after one p.m. the big jet landed in Washington. As we hurried toward the terminal I spotted Dad's sandy head towering above the crowd. He saw us and waved, "Michael, over here."

"Your Dad's a very dignified looking man". Jody exclaimed as my tall broad shouldered Father walked towards us, gave me a big bear hug and said, "Glad to have you home, son." He greeted Jody in the same friendly manner making her feel welcome.

"You have picked the most beautiful time of the year to visit us Jody, it is cherry blossom season now. I hope you both plan to stay with us for awhile."

"We can only stay for the weekend Father."

"Well, I guess that's better than not at all". He added.

"The reason your Mother is not here Michael, is that she and Helga are in the kitchen cooking up a storm."

I explained to Jody, "Helga has been working for us ever since I can remember. She's practically a member of the family."

"Let's hurry", Father said, "Mother is anxious to meet you Jody and to see Michael. He hasn't been home much lately."

Jody looked up at me and squeezed my hand as we walked to the car.

The drive home was relaxing but quiet. Soon our car drove off the highway and the large country estates rolled past us. We rode along until we came to the familiar country road which forked off into a private way that was flanked by a high stone wall.

The property was secluded by woods on both sides and after a few minutes we turned into a clearing and Jody's face glowed as she watched the horses grazing in the fields of beautiful green pastureland. We proceeded to cross over the small wood bridge that was over a brook and up an incline. I said, "We're here Jody," and pointed out my house in the distance. The car rolled through our heavy wrought iron gates and into Sonnenblume, the name Mother had given it many years ago which meant Sunflower. We drove around the fountain in the middle of the circular driveway and stopped in front of the house. Kempka, who was the family chauffeur since I was an infant and also the pilot of our family plane, took our two overnight bags. I watched as Jody nervously played with the lock on her clutch bag. Hearing her draw in a heavy breath I asked, "What's the matter?"

She whispered in my ear, "Michael, you didn't prepare me. I didn't realize you lived on an estate!" We walked across the wide veranda of the white Georgian Colonial and into the large reception hall with its twenty foot ceiling, held up by enormous pillars in each corner. I noticed Jody's eyes open as she looked up at the wide marble stairway and its hand carved railings, which I had been told, had been brought in from another country.

In fact the whole house had imported things from every part of the world that my folks had visited. From the oriental rugs to the Italian marble fireplaces to the priceless antiques and the hand carved wall panels.

"Erica, the children are here," Father called loudly. Mother came running into the hall in her usual high spirited manner and hugged and kissed me when Big Red, our beautiful Irish setter, spotted me, jumped up and licked my hands and face.

"Let me introduce you to Big Red, Jody." He obliged by putting his paw into her hand,

"Smart dog", I patted him as Mother looked at me. "Very nice to introduce the dog before your Mother!" she said smiling with her hands on her hips.

"Sorry Mother," I kissed her cheek. "This is Jody". "I'm glad to meet you Mrs. Ulricke," Jody said.

"And I'm happy to meet you. I hope you had a good trip." Mother said pleasantly as they kissed.

"Where is Grandfather," I asked, "Is he back from his trip?"

"He came home yesterday and was very excited to hear you were coming home.

Hopefully he will be back soon. He is at one of his usual meetings." Mother said sounding rather upset.

"Is he still active in all those clubs at his age?" I asked.

"Oh yes, he has many, many friends because when he wants to he can be very charming. You know your Grandfather." My Father remarked.

"Unfortunately," Mother continued, "he can't sit still. His mind is very active.

In fact, if birthdays did not come around every year we would never suspect his age.

Speaking of age I must not forget, next week April twentieth, is his birthday and the following week he starts jury duty."

Just then the door opened and my Grandfather came into the foyer. His dark hair, with touches of white, was neatly combed and his joy at seeing me reflected in his eyes, which sparkled beneath dark rimmed glasses. He came over, put his arms around me and we held each other close for a moment.

"Mein liebes kind". ('my beloved child) he said as the tears filled his eyes.

Turning, he spied Jody.

"And who is this lovely lady?" he asked. I realized then that my folks had not mentioned Jody at all. He took her hand into his, leaned over and kissed it.

"This is Jody Loeb, Grandfather. We are planning to be married." "Ya, so vot is da secret? No von told me."

"Who has had time to talk to you? As soon as you come home from South America, you are at one of your meetings!" Mother said angrily.

"Vot is the matter?" Grandfather asked. "You vant I should sit home in a rocking chair because I am going to be ninety-one years old? There are many people my age who still get around. Many famous ones like your Rose Kennedy, who is only a year younger than I and Marc Chagall, only a year older than I. So, let me do vot I vant, vhere and vhen I vant!"

Grandfather turned to Jody. "Your girl is a great looker, blue eyes like my wife had. I vant ve should be goot friends Jody, so ve vill start off vit you calling me 'Gramps', like Michael sometimes does." Grandfather loved an audience and as we walked into the library I could see he had already mesmerized Jody.

"Michael," he went on "is a vonderful boy, but you must not mind a Grandfather bragging. And you Jody, did anyvon ever tell you that your eyes are like sapphires?"

"No never but I love to hear it", she laughed as she said, "Gramps, I bet you had a way with the girls back home."

"In Germany I had a vay vit lots of people. There ver alvays many people around me, but", his voice saddened. "I did have a special voman in my life who shared all the goot days and she vas vith me through all my adverse times and ven"

"Father", my Mother interrupted, "the children need to freshen up from their trip and I'm sure they could use a little rest. They must be tired. Later when they come down we will talk again."

"Ya, vell in that case I vill vait."

Mother led us up to the guest rooms. On the way through the halls Jody stopped to admire the paintings on the wall.

"Those are Gramps, he's been painting ever since I can remember." "They are beautiful, he's very talented. I'll have to talk to him later

about art." Mother showed Jody to one of the many bedrooms which was very cheerful and feminine, done in yellow and lilac. A private bath was connected to it with a step down bathtub and from the bedroom French doors opened onto a small balcony that overlooked the rose garden and swimming pool.

"Mrs. Ulricke, this room is really lovely, in fact your whole house is, you have beautiful taste."

"Thank you Jody. Now why don't you rest up a bit from your trip and later Michael can show you around the house and grounds. I have a few errands to take care of this afternoon but I'll see you both in a little while, enjoy the afternoon. If there is anything you need just ring the bell by your bed."

Mother hurried off and Jody sank down into the big winged chair. "Tired?" I asked.

"On no, I guess I was very nervous over nothing, but I must admit I feel a little strange in such an enormous house."

"You will get use to the bigness". I assured her as I pulled her over to the small love seat and sat her on my lap.

"Your family seem very friendly, Michael. Are you sure they don't object to our marriage?"

"They not only do not object but they seem to like the girl I picked out. Besides they know I love you very much and that's all that's important to Mother and Dad. She looked at me for a few moments without talking. I pressed her close to me and we kissed.

"I love you Judith, very much."

"And I love you," she said as her lips gently kissed my face and I breathed in her fresh, clean smell.

"What do you think of the king size Henry VIII bed?" I asked. "I'm going to feel lost in it."

"I'll keep you company."

"I don't think that will happen here. You will have to wait." She said as she got up and started to examine the family pictures hanging on the wall.

"You know you don't look like your father, especially in this picture when he was younger. Your mother is the image of your grandfather. He's a very charming man."

"I know, he could charm the spots off a leopard. I love that character."

Jody started looking at my baby pictures. "Oh Michael, you were so adorable,

I would love to have a fat blonde baby like the one in this picture." She said lightheartedly.

"O.K. let's go to work on the great production!"

"I will not do that in the Henry the Eighth bed! Didn't he kill all his wives?

Now you go out and let me change and then I would love to see the horses and everything.”

“I’m more in the mood for something else.” I laughed. “Not here Mike.” she said as she held me at arms length. “That’s cruel.” I feigned deep hurt.

“Silly. Go down while I change into pants.” She laughed and pushed me out the door. Later we met in the library and walked through the house and out to the back where the horses were kept.

“This place is enormous Michael,” Jody remarked. “I think you could but my Mother’s whole apartment in half of the living room. You have so much land. It’s like having your own park. Your father must do very well working for the government.”

“It’s no that so much. I think my Grandfather has a lot of money.”

We ran across the fields to the pastures with Big Red at our heels as I waved to Ralph the stable boy.

“Alice is the only horse that I ever had who recognizes me and will come over without being offered something. Now let’s see if she remembers.”

“The words were hardly out of my mouth when the beautiful chestnut mare raised her head from the grass and gave a soft throaty noise and bolted across the field to where we were standing. She affectionately started to nuzzle my hand.

“Isn’t she a beauty, Jody? By the way, can you ride a horse?”

“No, I never learned. In fact, I’ve never been up on a horse. You forget, I’m a city girl from the Bronx. Remember?”

“Well, I’ll teach you this summer.” I guided Jody’s hand toward the animal. “Here, don’t be afraid always pet a horse on the neck first.” Suddenly, Alice opened her mouth wide and Jody jumped back.

“She won’t hurt you. She is a very mild tempered, gentle animal. I can even put my hand in her mouth.” I started to rub the horses gums as she made loving and soft throaty sounds.

"She's saying she is very happy." Jody grinned. "She should be. She is a lucky horse to be so well taken care of and to live in such a beautiful place and she even has you to rub her gums. She has real mazel!"

"We never muzzel Alice." I said.

"I know. She has a different kind of mazel. Spelled, m-a-z-e-l which in Jewish means 'Good Luck.'"

"Just having you Jody, is all the 'mazel' I need." I said as I bent over and kissed her. Before we realized it the afternoon had passed and we returned to the house. As we sat down to dinner my Mother remarked to Jody, "I hope you like German food. We have made all of Michael's favorite dishes."

"Oh I love it. But I could still use some of your recipes Mrs. Ulricke." "Well today we are going to have cabbage soup with dumplings and I

made Michaels favorite sauerbraten with spaetzle to take back to Boston. We baked some mandel kranze and a bienenstich, or as we say in English, an almond coffee cake."

The conversation was kept mostly to food until Jody said to Gramps. "I noticed your beautiful paintings hanging in the hall upstairs. They really are wonderful! Did you study art for many years?"

"Mostly I studied on my own. Ven I vas young I vould paint postcards and sell them but ven I could not get into Art School, that upset my whole life!"

"Oh Father!" Mother looked very disturbed. "It didn't upset your life.

You could still have become a successful artist, Chagall did!

"If only you had been accepted into art school," my Father commented sadly, "what a world of difference it would have made!"

"Well, it looks like Grandfather did alright anyway." I said trying to change the unhappy atmosphere. "You were a successful businessman. You know all the operas and have read every book one can think of that is of importance."

"I even wrote a book vunce! "Grandfather said proudly. "You never told me." I said anxious to hear more.

"He is joking." Mother interrupted.

"What about your family Jody?" My Father asked, changing the subject. "Do you have any brothers and sisters?"

"Unfortunately, I don't. I'm also an only child like Michael.

"Well, after a war was a hard time for people to think of having large families. There was very little money for most people and many were upset over losing loved ones." Mother said sympathetically.

"I remember, "Grandfather said laughing, "during the Nazi probe for Aryans and non Aryans, a joke vent around Germany."

"Father, it would be better without jokes tonight, please." Ignoring my mother he continued. "You recall the story of Little Red Riding Hood, Jody? Vell during the days of the Third Reich, they told the story this way. Little Red Riding Hood goes into the voods and is looking for her Grandmother, ven she meets the volf, he says to her, 'I too, am looking for my Grandmother, after all, who is not looking for their Grandmother these days?" Gramps laughed, but Jody replied coldly,

"I guess I'm not a good audience for that kind of a joke."

"Everybody had their troubles in those days." Mother interjected smiling. "Just a few months ago we had a reunion with the Kramer family. My parents had hidden them from the Nazis in our house at the risk of losing our lives. We never heard from them after they left to go to Switzerland. We thought, perhaps they were killed, but they did get to America, and after all these years they found us and we had a beautiful reunion with good Jewish friends! Unfortunately, Grandfather was away at the time."

A coughing sound came from next to me and I turned to see Gramps choking for breath. I patted him on the back and walked him around the room until he recovered. Just then the door opened from the kitchen and Helga wheeled in the tea cart.

"Oh everything looks so delicious." Jody remarked. "It's Mother's special diet desserts." I told her.

Mother asked, "Do you think my scher torte, make with apricot jam, whipped cream and chocolate frosting is for a diet Jody? I hope you appreciate Michael's sense of humor."

"Oh, I've gotten to understand it, Mrs. Ulricke but I don't know if I always appreciate it." She said as she looked at me with a twinkle in her eye. Never the less, we dug into the sweet delicious treats. Gramps patted Jody's head. "I see you are like Michael, you like goot German desserts."

"Yes, I could eat like this every day but I'd weigh a ton."

"There is only von vay to eat and be healthy. That is to be a vegetarian like me!" Gramps said. "I could never see how any von could eat an animal knowing it vas vunce a living breathing creature. I never smoke, that's vhy I am so strong and healthy at my age.

Michael, you should throw avay that pipe of yours. You are making a chimney of your body! You are inhaling soot!" After dinner we went into the living room and I put some more logs on the fire.

As Mother and Dad relaxed on the couch Jody walked over to the piano. I watched the flames leap up and cast shadows about her beautiful face as she started to play. Slowly, I walked over and sat down beside her and together we sang in German the words from Gustav Mollers, Your Two Blue Eyes. When we finished the family applauded and Grandfather started to talk about his favorite music.

"Do you know vot my favorite opera is Jody? Let me tell you, it is Vagner's, Rienzi! I could listen to Vagner for hours. Vagner eclipses Beethoven. He vas a spirit of sheer genius! I remember how, many years ago, I vould take ten days off every year to go to Festspielhaus in Bayreuth to listen to Vagners vorks. The Festspielhaus was built especially for Vagner's works. His opera Rienzi, is the most beautiful. It gave me most of my ideas and"

"Father!" My Mother exclaimed.

"I'm sorry, I guess I vas going on about myself, sometimes I forget. It is really you young people who should be talking about your plans. Just let me know ven the Church vedding vill be. It should be a beautiful vedding. Amen, Amen I say to that. Everybody vill come, spare no numbers! It vill be my gift to you children."

Jody gave me a questioning look when she heard 'Church wedding', but I just shrugged my shoulders and explained to Gramps. "We're planning a very small wedding Gramps, but thank you anyway."

"Vell that is up to you but either vay, I have a gift I put avay a long time ago for just such an occasion, goot night children."

"Well now," Mother started, "Jody you have not told us anything about yourself, although Michael tells us that you are a very talented girl."

"She certainly is." I said, "in fact she won a New York art contest a few months ago, and I'm sure after we are married if Jody decides to give up teaching she has great possibilities of becoming well known as an artist."

"Maybe you shouldn't be wasting a talent like that Jody." My Father said just as the front doorbell chimed and Uncle Ludwig, my Father's brother entered the room.

He was a tall, smiling man who had always remained close to the family. We had all hoped he would eventually marry but he remained a confirmed bachelor. I introduced Jody and he insisted she call him Uncle Ludwig and in a warm, friendly manner he inquired how we had met and about our plans. I was very happy to see my Uncle who came from Philadelphia, especially to see us and spend the weekend.

We all had coffee again but it was very late and everyone was tired. We planned to continue our visit with him the following day. As Jody and I walked to our rooms she told me she was disturbed by my Grandfather's talking about a Church wedding "and he knows I'm Jewish, doesn't he?"

"I don't think my folks told him." I said as I looked away from her eyes. "Well believe me, I'm telling him before I leave here. I'm not hiding anything. You know me better than that Michael!" "The only reason he wasn't told Jody is because"

"Because he would probably act just as my Father acted, right Michael?" "Listen Jody, let them all act as they want. I just don't want you to get any more aggravation from anyone like your family, my family, my Grandfather, anyone. Please, let's forget it." I took her into my arms and held her tight. I'm just trying to protect you Jody. I don't want anything to spoil things for us." "Oh Michael, Michael, I do love you so." Early the next morning Jody and

I had breakfast alone in the kitchen before anyone was awake, and left to go sightseeing. We spent the day like thousands of others and snapped pictures to take back to our pupils. The Washington Monument was the first on our list. Then we took in the Supreme Court Building, which resembles a white marble temple. Next we saw the elegant White House with the fountains and gardens. Before we came to Arlington House, where Robert E. Lee once lived, we found a spot on a hill to eat the delicious lunch Helga had packed for us the night before. For awhile we walked through the grass holding hands and just enjoying the smell of Cherry Blossoms and being together on this sun filled day.

Soon we were in Father's car again and we drove over to see the Lincoln and Jefferson Memorials. It was getting late but we were lucky and found a space to park not too far from the Capital. We arrived home early enough to play one set of tennis on our courts, and then had an early evening meal by the pool with Uncle Ludwig and some friends of the family. Father had just come back from his golf game at the club, with Gramps following him to the table, both hungry as bears.

After dinner Jody excused herself to take a bath and pack for our trip home while everyone tried to entice us to stay longer, especially Helga, who promised all kinds of tantalizing dishes. It was a short time later when Uncle Ludwig found me practicing some billiard shots in our library. He took a cue stick and joined me.

"We haven't had much chance to talk alone Uncle." I said as I shot the ball. "By the way things have progressed Michael, I think we should have talked together a lot more through the years." It was evident to me that Uncle

Ludwig was not his usual amiable self, so I put down my stick. "Is there something special on your mind?" I asked

"There certainly is!" He said as he seated himself in one of the overstuffed chairs. I walked over to the bar and poured us both a glass of bourbon.

"Michael, I do not want to interfere in your life, but you are the only nephew I have. You are like a son to me. So tell me, when you had such a wonderful career ahead of you in the Church and could have rose to such heights, yes even a Cardinal, anything could have been possible. Why? Why did you throw it all away? Was it because you met Jody?"

"No, it was way before I met her and there were many reasons. One reason was that I felt the single life was not for me. I wanted to marry. I wanted to have a family."

"So", Uncle Ludwig walked around the room with his hands folded together as he said, "that I can possibly understand, comprehend. But one thing I cannot understand and I cannot beat around the bush. Tell me, you who have so much to offer a girl and could have had the cream of the crop, girls whose backgrounds are more like ours, why a Jewish girl?"

I stood up, "Why not a Jewish girl!" I said angrily. "Our Christian life is wrapped around the religion of Jody's ancestors!"

"I know all my history Michael, my dear nephew." he said in an exasperated tone as his face clouded and he concentrated on the cue ball. "Jody seems like a lovely girl," he paused while I waited. "You know Michael, as soon as I heard you were getting married I planned on making you and your wife life members in my Greenwood Country Club, but let's face it, you will not get in married to someone like her."

"Uncle, pardon my expression but fuck your country club!" I got up from the chair and started to leave the room.

"Wait, wait a minute, Michael. You don't understand." he said as he quickly dropped his cue stick and walked over to me.

"I understand well. I understand that this anti-Semitic gangrene is being kept alive by people like you!"

"Michael, you don't know what you're saying. You're love sick."

"It's you that's sick, dear Uncle. You have that sickness, that cancer   of the heart, which helped Hitler build Nazism and led to World War II. That sickness, which poisons minds and rots hearts and caused the death of more people in that war than in all the wars of history put together, without counting the Jews!"

"Michael, as far as history, you are probably right but you are not correct about me! I have many Jewish friends. I am even president of the Greenwood Country Club's Board of Brotherhood! Why even Rabbi Ben Cohen commented on the clubs Christmas/ Chanukah program that I helped run which was open to everyone."

The pulse in my temples pounded as I said, "Ah, come on Ludwig, stop the bullshit! Your country club is full of bigots. Why else won't they allow Jews, blacks, Orientals and Moslems? What's the use, I must be blunder hund (real stupid) to try and reason with you."

"What about those other country clubs that only welcome their own religious brothers? There are clubs that only welcome Jews!"

"You know how I feel about that. Discrimination and segregation are no damn good! They only help prejudice live on. They preserve it and nourish it!" I went quickly to the door.

"Michael, Michael," he ran over to me. "lets forget the past. Let's forget religion. That's not what I wanted to talk about. It's your life in which I am really, sincerely interested. I don't want you to make mistakes that you will be sorry for later. Let's talk man to man." He pulled out a chair for me, and foolishly I sat down and listened. "Michael, you are a very intelligent young man. You are well read. You know your history. But the world of today you don't seem to know very well. Unfortunately, you don't seem to know much about women and you think I don't know much either but I do! I've had my experiences. You I will tell."

I looked up at him as he rose from his chair and stood across from me rubbing his hands together and smiling as he said, "Let me give you a little advice. Enjoy yourself. Live with her. She may be a very talented bed mate. But you don't have to marry her not in today's world!"

I got up from my chair and said, "But I intend to marry Judith! We are in love something you may never know and never feel. And we will have children that will be raised without hate and vengeance imbued inside them."

Ludwig's face was flushed and he walked toward the French doors and stared outside. Eventually he turned to me and said with a smile, "Well Michael, one thing I must say for you. She is a beautiful girl. She doesn't even look Jewish."

"What's a Jew suppose to look like Uncle? If you're referring to the hooked nose, the dark hair, short stature and emotional temperament, you may as well be describing Grandfather!"

"Is somevon calling me?" Gramps walked into the room.

"Uncle Ludwig and I were discussing a few popular subjects, like Jews, anti-semitism, bigots, and Hitler." I said.

"Vell, I vill join the discussion. On those subjects I am vell read and vell versed. Amen to that!"

Uncle Ludwig absorbed himself in peeling an orange from the fruit bowl and breaking the skin into atomic pieces. It was obvious he was struggling to retain an outward calm. Grandfather started to speak.

"Actually the Nazis used anti-Semitism to help them rise to power. Hatred of Jews vas international and Hitler knew that he could use this tool to get the anti-Semites of the vorld to support him."

"Listen Ludwig, listen carefully," I said as Gramps continued. "Hitler despised communism, humanism, intellectualism, the enlightenment, free thought, and the Jews.

Hitler saw the Nazi movement as a bulwark against communism and

Russia. Remember Michael, Hitler did not lie about vot he vas going to do. His book, Mein Kampf, vas very clear about vat he planned. Everyvon read his book and he made himself a million dollars. Hitler vanted to unite the vorld into von Reich vhere his German Supermen vould rule the people and over all vould be von Fuhrer."

"That's right," I said, "He took Nietzsche's Superman Theory, and used it against the Jews since they had already been made the scapegoat throughout history so it was easy for him."

Gramps went on, "Hitler said to the people that God sent him but he really had no use for God or the church. He fooled the masses that listened to his hypnotic voice. Adolph vas smart, some people even say brilliant!"

"He was a psychopath!" I said in no uncertain terms. A psychopath's life is dominated by the need to immediately satisfy any desire he has and to go to any lengths to do it. That's why so many of them become criminals. Hitler was dominated by an excessive need for power. A psychopath like Hitler portrays a facade of trust and superficial warmth. That is how Hitler became the Nazi leader. A psychopath like Hitler is capable of selling his ideas to people even when those ideas are wrong through his ability to interpret them in such a way as to make them sound rational. It was through these means that Hitler had millions of Jews and millions of Christians killed. Since a psychopath is not capable of experiencing the feeling of guilt or remorse for the suffering of others. Men with syphilitic thinking like Hitler have been allowed to become leaders in the past and can become leaders in the future."

As if he never heard, Grandfather raised his right hand and shouted on high,

"Gut mit unz, (God with us) that is vat Hitler taught his army. He pretended his great love for the church and used the people. He preached the three K's which were Kinder, Kirche and Kuche. (Children, Church and Kitchen) And here in America now there is another group vit the three K's who haff become more and more active every year. They are the Ku Klux Klan and they haff no love for Jews, Blacks or Catholics. But let us go back in time." Grandfather continued. The people ver stupid, they thought that Hitler shared the same ideas as they, such as not vanting abortion."

"But most military dictatorships do not want birth control anyway because they want to raise soldiers." I said, as Grandfather went on involved in his story.

"Back in Italy, Pacelli, who later became Pope Pius XII, vas fooled by Hitler, and talked Pius XI, into signing the Concordat vit Nazi Germany in July of 1933. By doing this it showed the country that they accepted Hitler and so tventy million Catholics became Nazis. In Germany the entire Catholic Parliament on the recommendation of their trusting priests who ver also fooled by Hitler, passed the Enabling Act, vich took their power away, and gave it to Hitler!"

"They were duped." I said, "Hitler then did away with democracy and became the sole dictator of Germany."

"Hitler told the people to lead the vay in being goot patriots and to serve the Reich vit all their hearts and souls. The people believed and listened to Hitler and he devised a Military Oath for the Nazi armed forces and again used religion. It read, 'I svear by God this Holy Oath, that I vill render unconditional obedience to the leader of the German Reich, Adolf Hitler, Supreme Commander of the Armed Forces, and that as a brave soldier, I vill be ready at any time to stake my life for this Holy Oath.

I turned to Uncle Ludwig, "See, people were made into puppets. A dictatorship of murderers took over the German government. They used a theological hatred of the Jews, from centuries ago, to unite their people, who ended up suffering and dying themselves from the war or were put in the death camps of Auschwitz, Dachau, Feblinko and others, alongside the Jews." I noticed an eerie, unexplainable look that passed between Ludwig and Grandfather and a peculiar feeling crept over me. Grandfather poured a little sherry for himself and I could see his hands tremble as he said in a confident voice, "Nothing changed after World Var I and I do not see vhere anything

has changed since the devastation of Vorld Var II."

"Unfortunately, the madness of Nazism is rising again." I said. "The Nazi march on a street in Chicago is not too different from a strasse in Berlin, many years ago. The Triple K and Nazism both march to the tune of the same drummer. That is the tune of 'hate' which is a very unifying emotion and Hitler knew it."

"The Nazis ver told by Alfred Rosenberg and Goring to preach a beautiful hate to bind the vorld together. Hate, is the tool, not love. It is hate!" Grandfather said knowingly. I drew in a deep breath and said, "It's all true Gramps, and you remember all the details. What really is sad is that the world learned little from World War Two. It's no smarter now than it was in your day Grandfather."

"So tell me Michael, you seem to know all the answers," Ludwig started, "why don't you do something about this? Every time I pick up a newspaper I see some story about the Nazis or the Ku Klux Klan."

"That's because there are too many people like you around Ludwig, and because many people who believed and supported Nazism before were not killed off. Wealthy Nazis escaped and were taken in by friends all over the world and have now raised another generation of people who believe as they do. These Nazis have recently been involved in many violent acts against Jews and have been giving out their anti-Semitic newspaper, White Power, in every country. This new generation is called, The Fourth Reich, and it has over one hundred organizations in the United States alone that send propaganda to all corners of the world. They are even writing books denying six million Jews were killed and falsifying conditions that really existed in their concentration camps.

There are Nazi candidates running for public office on the National Socialist Party ticket in cities throughout the United States and they are getting more votes every year!"

"Ya?" Grandfather said. "Imagine letting Nazis, vit the beliefs they have, run in a public election! People are as blind today as the readers of Mein Kampf ver not so many years ago."

"People have already forgotten the millions of Christians that were killed by the Nazis." I said. "We are lucky Ludwig that there were people without hate, like Grandfather in Germany who were members of the Resistance." Ludwig glared at us with narrowed eyes but continued to sit and listen as I continued. "There was the curate Rodel, the Jesuit Alfred Delp and Franz Steffen, the journalist who were all members of the Resistance who were put to death resisting the Nazis. You see Ludwig, there were and still are decent people without hate, people like our family. Without them and others in the Resistance more Christians and Jews would have been killed! You see the evils of hate, cruelty, persecution, intolerance, concentration camps, funeral pyres and massacres of people go back to the ancient pagan world and were used by empire builders for centuries.

These means were waiting to be used again by Hitler. He just continued to use what was already there! Any leader with enough influence can still use it because hate like yours Ludwig is still around but this time, with today's weapons it may cause the final field of blood and the last golgotha of our civilization. People like you Ludwig are spiritually back in antiquity even though they fly jets!" I said angrily as I accidentally pushed over the little table with several glasses, which crashed to the floor.

At that moment, Mother entered exclaiming, "Michael! Ludwig! Father! For shame! The servants will think we are crazy! Such arguing and yelling! The three of you are not going to change the world!"

"My daughter is right." Gramps said. "She is always right!"

"Mother, I am sorry about the raised voices, but the world has its head and heart in the stone age."

"I just do not want the servants in on a family dispute." Mother reminded us. She pulled my head down and kissed me. "I cannot be angry with you too long Michael, but why on such a short visit do you have to upset Uncle Ludwig? He was looking forward so much to seeing you. Look at Grandfather, look how excited he is. His blood pressure will go up! If we are not careful he can have a stroke!"

At this time Jody came down with Kempka carrying our overnight bags as

Mother continued, "If you have something important to say Michael why don't you just write it in your book?"

"I did write it in my book Mother, in fact, I've completed the book and sent it in."

"Michael," Jody came over to me, "why didn't you say anything about it before this?"

"Well, I didn't want anyone to get their hopes up. It just so happened that I met an editor from a large publishing company last month who told me to send him my manuscript. He didn't make me any promises. Remember Jody, how I worked every night at the typewriter?"

"Yes, but I didn't realize you had finished the book! Do you think you will hear from him soon?"

"It could take a month or six months, and then they may not want it, but this editor seemed very interested."

"What's the book about?" Ludwig asked.

"It's about everything you don't want to know, don't want to believe and don't want to read. But Ludwig you will read it because you will be curious." I smiled to myself.

Jody went over and said goodbye to my Uncle and Gramps who walked beside her as we all went to the front door where he said, "One question I vould like to ask you," Gramps smiled. "Vhere did you get the name Jody?" "It's just a nickname like 'Gramps.' My full name is Judith Sharon.

I was named after both my Grandmothers. My Jewish name is Yehudith Shoshanah."

I noticed the smile disappear from Grandfather's face and he suddenly looked grim. I was about to say something when Mother quickly took Judith's arm and mine and literally pulled us out of the doorway and into the circular driveway where the car was waiting with Kempka, behind the wheel. Father helped Jody into the car and told Kempka to drive carefully. Mother kissed us and we waved goodbye.

Later as we settled back in our seats and the plane took off Jody sighed deeply. I took her hand in mine as she said. "I guess your Grandfather won't be at our wedding now that he knows I'm Jewish."

"Really Jody, I don't understand it." I told her. "His attitude certainly was odd.

Sometimes age can do strange things to people.

"But he had a terrible expression when he heard I was Jewish. And then your Mother pulled us out to the car so quickly." Jody continued very agitated. "Forget it Jody. We are not going to change anything by talking about it.

Maybe someday", I said dreamily, "if my book gets published it will change a few viewpoints that people

"Do you think it has a chance, Michael?"

"It probably would have a better chance if it were a love story," I grinned, "but I heard that even Gone with the Wind was turned down sixteen times,"

"The parts I read in your book were wonderful." "You're biased, Jody."

"Oh Michael, everything was almost perfect."

"Jody we knew when we made our decision it wasn't going to be easy. Why don't you just plan the wedding now. Call up that place in Rockport on the ocean that you liked for the ceremony and just think of where you would like to go for a honeymoon. We have to make reservations. It's only two months away."

She leaned her head against my arm as the plane sped through the sky.

Then she turned to me, her face brightened.

"You always know the right things to say to me Michael."

"That's because I know you," I whispered in her ear, "and I love the you I know."

SEVENTEEN

A Very Private Celebration

It was ten o'clock Sunday night when we finally arrived at our apartment weary and tired from the trip, we fell right to sleep. The sound of the doorbell woke us up as sunlight streamed into our bedroom

"What time is it?" Jody squealed, covering her head with the pillow. I pushed my head under it alongside hers.

"It's eleven o'clock and someone's at the door." "Don't answer it, maybe they'll go away."

"It may be important. I'd better go see."

"But Michael I thought you were suffering from sexual malnutrition." "I am, but I will abstain until I return and then I will demand squatters

rights," I said laughingly. I put on my robe and on opening the door found Mrs. Kravitz.

"Oye Vay, please, disturbing you I must be." She said as she eyed my bathrobe. "I vill another day come."

"Don't you dare leave Grandma Kravitz." I said pulling her into the apartment.

"Bringing you only some mail I am. To me the post office sent the wrong address and maybe for you it vas important I felt."

Grandma handed me two letters. One had the return address of the publishing house I had sent my book. Quickly I tore open the envelope.

"Jody", I yelled, "Jody, come here." She rushed into the room as she tied the belt of her bathrobe together.

"Hello Grandma", she said as she kissed her.

"Look, look at what they wrote." "Who wrote to you?"

"The publishing company wants to publish my book!" Jody read the letter as I swung Grandma Kravitz around the room.

"Michael, getting dizzy I am! But so happy I am." Jody jumped up and hugged me. "Michael it's wonderful. Grandma isn't it wonderful?"

"Now, people famous I can say I know. But maybe so famous you vill get, no more I vill see you."

"That will never happen, Grandma." We sat down next to her. "We will never forget you because it was you who brought us the good news."

"Now, I feel like my own children you are and away you vill go and when vill I see you again?" She sniffled into her handkerchief.

"Grandma, we love you. You will always see us and besides, we're not famous yet, and we're not going anywhere." Jody told her.

"I do have to go to New York, Jody. They want to talk to me about the book and a contract, but tonight we are all going to celebrate, all three of us!"

"You vant I should go vit you?"

"Of course we want you to go with us Grandma." Jody told her, "And mine hair I can haff done and mine new dress I can vear and"

"And we will pick you up tonight at six o'clock sharp." I told her. I put on some coffee while Jody started making some waffles for all of us. "It's no trouble", she insisted to Grandma,

"There is nothing like a good healthy, hot breakfast, besides this is a special occasion." She said as she popped the frozen waffles into the toaster.

"You young people vit instant this, vit instant that."

"Well you brought us instant happiness this morning Grandma." Jody told her.

"Happy you ver before instant success you became. Alvays, you remember!" "We will Grandma." I yelled from the bedroom as I pulled on my pants

to drive her home.

During the day I called Charles and let him knew the good news. My family was also very happy but when Jody called her Mother the conversation drifted to other things and it put a damper on her spirits. Soon the news spread and Dr. Ling called. Before I knew it we had a party of six going out with us.

It was going to be a big celebration. But meanwhile Jody was waiting for a private celebration in the bedroom so I dropped my pants.

Jody put out her arms to me and I covered her body with mine, just as a ringing sound broke through the silence.

"Oh not the doorbell again !" She said. As I pulled on my pants I thought to myself these pants are getting plenty of action but I'm certainly not. I opened the door.

"Flowers by Joseph," the young man said as he handed me the large box. "Jody," I called, "we've got flowers."

"Fine", she yelled, "Now we just need music. So bring in your organ!" Again I pulled off my pants and started for the bedroom with the flowers. "Oh Michael, the flowers are beautiful, but your stem is wilting." She

laughed.

I climbed into bed and Jody started cultivating my stem. "Michael, do you think I have a green thumb?"

"Honey, I don't know about your green thumb but you sure can make it rain during the dry season!"

"Michael, I once read that to get the best results from plants one must give the preparation of the soil adequate attention."

"If you continue your preparation of my soil Jody, I believe we will soon have a Giant Begonia. Would you like me to give you a giant begonia ?"

"Michael honey, it's what I've always wanted and I have the perfect place for it." She said as I moved up into her garden path. We were under the covers, my face warm in her body, her body shaking with delight. The hot burning sensations felt good after all these day. We rocked back and forth, back and forth.

"Michael, take out your begonia", she cried. "It's beginning to germinate." "But it feels so good Jody."

Reluctantly, I pulled out my Begonia.

"Michael, put it back, back to the soil!" I quickly put a terrarium over my flower. Gently I went up her garden path and into her greenhouse. It was hot in there and I began to sweat.

"Feel me good now Jody?"-

"Oh Mike you're stem has grown. It's so straight and tall. It feels like it's in full bloom!" It seemed like hours had gone by. We had slept, had awakened and made love again. I kissed her fragrant auburn hair, her shapely legs, her petal white stomach, her dainty appendix stitches, her glowing full round flowering breasts, her rose-like nipples.

Again I placed my stalk into position and again it began to flourish. The phone rang. It rang again. I reached for the receiver as I jogged along.

"Western Union is calling. We have a telegram message for Mr. Ulricke. "This is Mr. Ulricke speaking.

"Congratulations on your book. Stop. May you always be successful in whatever you attempt. Stop. signed, Principal Bradshaw. Stop."

"I hung up the phone, and looked down at my last attempt. My hardy Tiger Lily had become a wilting violet. Jody slid on top of my body and in my ear she planted the seeds of thought which led us into the land of paradise again.

That evening, at the restaurant we all enjoyed a boisterously funny party.

Doctor Ling and Grandma Kravitz hit it off right away. Within half an hour they came to a first name relationship and from then on it was 'Sadie' and 'Harold' all evening. Between Grandma with her 'oye vay', Dr. Ling with his Confucius and Mary Ann's southern drawl, we thought the waiter would go mad just trying to get the orders from the table.

We laughed, we danced and we toasted my book until the wee hours of the morning.

The next day Grandma Kravitz called,

"So happy I vus vit Harold Ling. Making me feel like Madam Chung Kie Sheck, he did. Ven home to the door he took me, Oye Vay, like a queen I felt ven over mine hand he bent to giff a kiss! So beautiful a man he is. If a little younger he vould be, under mine bed his shoes could go anytime!"

"Grandma", I kidded her, "he is a few years younger." Not wanting to mention he was at least fifteen years her junior.

"Michael, last night I vas feeling twenty years younger, so don't argue!

Just be lucky vit the book!"

The following week I went to the publisher's office and signed a contract.

EIGHTEEN

A Day To Remember

The month of June was now upon us, with school closing and parties given in honor of our marriage by the faculty, friends and fellow teachers. It was a hectic but happy time in our life.

Sunday, June twenty-sixth, our wedding day finally arrived. I was awakened by the sunshine which streamed in through my bedroom window. Suddenly, Jody had become old-fashioned and decided to stay the last few days before the wedding with Grandma Kravitz, especially since her mother was flying in a couple of days prior to the affair. My best man, Charles, Mary Ann and I arrived early at the Seaside Villa in Rockport, where our wedding was to take place. We had decided this villa overlooking the ocean was the most beautiful of all the places we had seen. The ocean and Rockport were very significant to us since it was on these very sands where Jody and I had first declared our love. The grounds were surrounded by beautiful lawns and on the terrace side a large tent had been set up overlooking the ocean, which would be the

background for our entire wedding ceremony and reception.

Inside the tent yellow gladiolus with yellow bows lined both sides of the aisle. The orchestra was arriving and some of the guests were already seating themselves. I kept looking at my watch. Jody hadn't arrived and it was getting late. Tony handed me a drink to calm my nerves and telephoned Grandma Kravitz's apartment but there was no answer.

Cynthia came over to me a few minutes later and told me Jody had just arrived through the side door with her Mother, Aunt and Uncle, but that I wasn't allowed to see her before the ceremony.

Tony put me in a room where Charles and a few other men sat drinking and joking about my losing my bachelorhood, while Mary Ann fluttered back and forth from Jody's room to mine checking on us both.

Ludwig didn't look too happy but seemed to be making the best of it to the extent of having a pre-nuptial schnapps with the Rabbi and Priest. We had planned an ecumenical wedding to try and please both sides of our family as much as possible, and were lucky to find two clergymen who did not want to 'turn off' anyone from their respective religions by refusing to marry them.

With noontime only a few seconds away the Priest glanced at his wristwatch and gave the signal for everyone to be seated. The Rabbi joined him and soon the theme from Romeo and Juliet better known as the song 'A Time For Us', filled the air. It was now time for me to walk down the isle and stand under the canopy to await my bride. Finally I heard the familiar strains of the Wedding March, and Jody appeared. She looked even more beautiful than I imagined she would and I heard soft gasps of admiration as she walked down the isle toward me, radiant and smiling. Her gown matched the three long stemmed yellow roses that she carried and her gorgeous auburn hair fell on the yellow shawl she had spent so much time crocheting. I saw her Mother give her a loving smile and a moment later wipe away her tears. Jody's Father had not appeared but Uncle Abe was there to take his place and give the bride away. My own parents had risen to the occasion and looked happy enough, only Ludwig stood there grim. Jody had chosen Cynthia as her matron of honor and her cousin little Sherman, was the ring bearer. We gave Grandma Kravitz the honor of walking down the isle as our adopted Grandmother, on the arm of Cynthia's husband Tony. She glowed almost as much as my bride. Now everyone was together around the canopy and the Rabbi started with the ceremony that Jody and I had written.

"We are gathered here today to join together Judith and Michael in marriage.

This ceremony is the outward symbol of an inward union which already dwells in the hearts of these two people. Judith and Michael have chosen to journey together on this earth, bound as one by their love, yet free as the waves of the sea to make their separate marks on the sands of time."

The Priest added,

"May you both seek and find a growing relationship which will blend you together physically, mentally and spiritually. May this relationship flower and grow into a garden of beauty; and may it flow from you both and influence everything around you."

Now Jody and I took turns speaking responsively. "I, Judith, take you Michael, to be my husband." "I, Michael, take you Judith, to be my wife.'

Jody and I then said together:

"I promise to stand beside and with you always, in times of gladness and times of sadness, in times of pain and times of health. I will live with you and love you as long as we are one, as long as we both shall live."

We then presented our rings to each other as the Rabbi said,

"The circle of the ring is as love freely given, it has no beginning and it has no end."

Judith and I both drank from the same cup of wine, symbolic of unity, which the Rabbi gave us as he said,

"Drink now, and may your lives be enriched in the joy of fulfillment, as this full cup of wine is symbolic of happiness."

The Priest then gave a Benediction:

"True marriage must contain the inward bond of trust and love which now dwells in the hearts of Judith and Michael. Only they will know what marriage exists between them. The outer forms are only signs and covers over the love of their hearts. We who are gathered here wish for you a happy marriage. We pray that you may find together richness beyond the wealth of money. A depth of being that will make beautiful everything you do in life, individually and in togetherness. With mutual joy in our hearts we send you off with our deepest blessings. Judith and Michael, having chosen one another from the many men and women of the earth, and having made your pledges to one another I hereby pronounce you both husband and wife."

The Rabbi then said:

"In our tradition the breaking of the glass in our greatest moment of joy, at a wedding, recalls the sorrow in the history of our people, when the two great Temples of Jerusalem were demolished and over six million of our people and millions of others were destroyed by the holocaust. It is symbolic of new hope that these terrible events will never happen again."

I then stamped my foot down and broke the glass and everyone said in unison,

"Mazel Tov ! Good Luck!"

I kissed Jody. The band played our song 'There's A Place in My Heart', as I walked back up the isle with her on my arm to the receiving line where we were congratulated and kissed by everyone.

A few minutes later Charles proposed a toast in front of the magnum of champagne which was bubbling in a huge bowl in the center of the hors d'oeuvre table. Everyone lifted their drinks and I clasped Jody's hand tightly as we raised our glasses along with the others.

"To Mike and Jody," Charles started in his booming voice, "may all their wishes come true and may they have a long and happy life together."

The cheerful sound of friendly voices, laughter and glasses clinking continued and the doors leading to the circular garden terrace were opened to expose tables with flowered umbrellas placed around the patio. It was a perfect day for an outdoor wedding.

The waiters walked around and served hot and cold appetizers, while some guests enjoyed the bar at the far side of the terrace and where the men were now leading me. Charles was already there crying 'Bottoms Up' every two minutes to Mary Ann. Standing next to him was Doctor Ling who had his arm around Grandma swaying to the music of the band.

I managed to get back to Jody after having another drink. She was standing with her Mother and Aunt Frieda. She had a painful, hurt look on her face and her eyes were filled with tears.

"Never you mind your Father! You just be happy." Frieda said. She took my hand and Jody's. "As long as two beautiful people like you had the sense to fall in love, I do not want anything to spoil this day of days for you!" Her mother kissed us both and said to me "Please take good care of my daughter, my only daughter." As my Mother and Father joined us I remarked, "I see Grandfather couldn't make it."

"He's very old Michael, much too old to go running around like he has been doing. It is better he didn't come. The excitement could have been too much for him." she said trying to cover up.

Just then Jody's friend Bernie came over with his Mother and Father.

Bernie shook my hand, put his other arm around my shoulders and said, "No hard feelings, I just hope the best man won." as he walked away.

It was very obvious to me that Bernie's family had wanted Jody for their daughter-in-law from the sad but tender way they looked when they kissed her. "Ve have known Judith's family from the old country, and Judith, since

the day she vas born. Ve hope you vill make each other very happy." Bernie's Father, Doctor Goldberg shook my hand.

"What about the whoopee?" Mary Ann came over and asked, "That is on the honeymoon!" Charles laughed,

"No," Mary Ann persisted, "ah heard when ah Rabbi has a wedding there's always a 'whoopie'. The Rabbi heard Mary Ann's words and moved over to us to explain.

"She means a 'chupah', that was the canopy which you saw Jody and Michael stand under when they took their vows. It is supposed to lend an atmosphere of royalty to the occasion, for the bride and groom are considered king and queen on their wedding day. It is also a symbol of the privacy to which the newly-wed couple is entitled. In ancient times it was meant to be a bridal chamber."

"Thank ya Rabbi but there is one other thing that ah must ask ya about."
"Careful Mary Ann", Charles warned.

"Oh Charles, don't go an get nervous. Ah am not going ta ask the Rabbi about sex. Ya seem ta think that is the only thing ah can discuss lately!"

"There is nothing wrong with discussing sex, Mary Ann." The Rabbi said.

"Do you really mean that? Ya know you are the first Rabbi that ah have ever heard even mention it!"

"There is nothing shameful about sex. It's a very beautiful thing." the Rabbi continued.

Ya hear that Charles! Rabbi ah would love ta have ah long discourse with ya one day on that subject. Ah hope ah won't embarrass ya if ah say that ah think ya are ah very cute Rabbi." Mary Ann smiled and patted his beard. "Ah love Rabbi's with little goatees. It tickles when they kiss ya."

"Mary Ann !" Charles glared at her.

"Well ta get back ta ma original question, before ma fiance explodes.

What is a 'chaley'? Someone told me Jewish people make blessings over something called a 'chaley' that they eat."

"That my dear, was the large loaf of Jewish bread you saw on the table. It is called a 'challah'. Wasn't it delicious?" the Priest asked, as both clergymen waved goodbye to everyone.

Grandma said happily, "I baked it mineself, vit raisins, so for all their life sveetness they should have." and she danced off with Dr. Ling to do the Hully Gully.

Slipping her hand into mine Jody pulled me over to the food. We had platters filled with a variety of summer salads while a chef stood at the table and served charcoal, broiled brochette of seafood cooked over hot glowing coals. The wedding cake was rolled out by little Sherman and a dessert table filled with miniature cakes and every summer fruit imaginable was placed beside it. The music played and Jody and I danced our first dance together as husband and wife. I brushed her cheek against mine. "I love you liebchen," I said and kissed her. Applause came from our friends who joined us on the dance floor. Even the waves sounded like they were dancing as they splashed against the shore. Unnoticed, we slipped upstairs and changed our clothes to leave. A half hour later we kissed everyone goodbye. Jody's Mother took me aside and said,

"Please take good care of our daughter. She is all we have in the world and she is everything to both of us, even though her Father didn't come to the wedding."

Jody threw her bouquet over the railing and jubilant Mary Ann screamed out with delight as she caught it. Outside we found our new Thunderbird completely decorated with streamers and a big 'Just Married' sign. We waved to everyone as the sun was beginning to set and started off for the little island beach house we had rented in Maine for our honeymoon.

NINETEEN

The Island Of Love

The noise of city life was left behind and we looked forward to lazy days without television, radio, newspapers or the Rowley School, to upset us. We arrived on the island by a small speed boat which had been left with the boat attendant at the dock. After the short ride across the lake we walked up the path to the beach house with our two suitcases in hand. It was already dark and deadly silent except for the ripple of the waters, the scurrying of small animals in the woods, the croaking of frogs and the call of the birds. We approached the small beach house and I unlocked the front door.

"Michael, what are you doing?" screamed Jody as I lifted her up in my arms. "You married an old fashioned guy. I believe in carrying my bride over the threshold." She laughed as we entered the comfortable looking house which was simply furnished and very welcoming. It had a wood paneled living room with a fireplace, a dining area and modern kitchen as one large room with sliding, glass doors that opened to a sundeck which overlooked the lake. The two bedrooms were completely surrounded by woods.

"Michael, I love it! I could live here forever!" she said as she flopped down on the rattan couch in front of the fireplace. The temperature had dropped and the house felt chilly. I found some logs stacked in a small closet and started a fire blazing. Jody took off her shoes and started looking around for food.

"Michael the refrigerator is stocked and so are the cabinets just like the owner promised."

"Good, I'm hungry", I said as I dragged her over to the couch." Jody nestled in my arms but as I started nibbling at her earlobes she pulled me down in front of the blazing fireplace onto the soft shag rug. My lips caressed the back of her neck as my hands moved up and down her body gradually unbuttoning her blouse. I felt her breasts and the beautiful pink nipples that stiffened as I touched them. Slowly we eliminated each piece of clothing from our bodies until we both lay there completely nude on the rug. She intoxicated me as I looked at her and I buried my face between her breasts, tasting   her hard nipples with my tongue. I felt the warmth of her response as she turned, twisted and swayed in complete abandonment. Up and down I moved in rhythm with her as she gasped with pleasure. Confidently, I continued my love making conscious only of the ravaging, throbbing sensations that engulfed me to a frenzy and then left me with a rapturous contentment.

We slept there on the rug as the sound of the wind howled and the logs cracked.

Our next two weeks together were so wonderful that it never entered my mind that things could change. Some mornings we awoke at dawn and listened and watched the woodpeckers that hammered at the trunk of a tree just outside our window as their babies waited with open mouths for their breakfast, We walked through the woods listening to the early morning chattering of the birds and inhaled the clean smells of the earth, the birch and pine trees and the flowers that grew wild. On the sun deck we barbecued steaks, drank beer and listened to some of our favorite tapes that we had taken along with our little recorder. During the days we spent our time under the big yellow ball in the sky. The noonday sun was so intensely hot that we both stripped bare and ran into the lake together,

"You look mighty sexy romping in the water without clothes." I said as I grabbed at her nice round rear and sat her in the water between my legs.

"Michael you don't want to do it here, do you?"

"Yes! Let's do it right here now in front of all the fish, the birds and the animals. Come Jody, hold me tight and don't let the water pull you away.

Don't let anything ever pull you away, never ever, promise me!"

"Michael, you're so serious. What's the matter? You know nothing can ever take me away from you. You are everything to me! You always will be. You should know it Michael!" and she kissed me hard on the lips.

Several hot nights we went midnight swimming. I dived after Jody when she went underwater with a great deal of skill. We came up for air and I asked her, "Where did a city girl like you ever learn to swim like that?"

"At the Fulton Avenue Y, "she answered laughing. She swam through my legs and I swam through hers while making love to her body underwater. Her white flesh shined in the moonlight and we dried ourselves without towels by rubbing our bodies against one another. She wrapped her hands tightly around my neck and lifted her face to kiss me. The next thing I knew we were stretched out on the sand, her beautiful red hair falling long and loose against her body.

Everyday Jody sat awhile and did some sketches. Happily planning to frame them and hang them in our apartment. She sketched everything from the frogs in the lake to me standing in the nude.

"That one you are not hanging on the wall!" I told her.

Early one morning while Jody slept I crawled out of bed and went fishing. At seven a.m. I was back and when Jody awoke she was greeted by a beautiful big trout staring at her.

"Michael, how you've changed." she laughed, "you even smell different." "Here I am trying to get a rise out of you Jody, and instead I get early morning good humor," I put the fish in the refrigerator and crawled back into bed, fish smell and all. But at this Jody didn't laugh. She threw me out of the

bed, hit me with the pillows and told me to take a shower.

Before we realized it, a week and a half had passed. The time was going too fast. We stood together looking at the luminous rainbow the sun cast on the rippling waves. Then strolling barefoot along the shore I thought to myself what life would have been like had I stayed in the Priesthood never to know what sharing a life with a woman you loved was like. I hugged Jody tightly against me.

"I love you, Liebling, more than anyone or anything in the world." And to myself I thought as I watched two squirrels scamper through the trees after each other, they're smarter than a lot of people.

The night before we left the island I went for a swim alone since Jody was tired. When I returned and walked into the darkened bedroom I smelled something foul. I went over to the open window and whiffed the air, but it didn't seem to come from the outside.

As I climbed into bed, Jody moved her body closer to me. The odor was unbearable! It smelled like rancid cheese and salami mixed with fried turd! I wondered if Jody had been sick and thrown up. She nuzzled her head up to me but the stench was unbearable.

"Michael, did you have a good swim?"

"Yes, it was very nice. Are you feeling alright, Jody?"

"I'm fine." she answered. I didn't mention anything to her about the smell but I moved over and turned on the light. I couldn't believe it was the same girl!

"What in hell have you got plastered all over your face? It stinks to high heaven!"

"Oh goodness," she cried out as her hands went up to her cheeks. "I fell asleep with the face pack on I forgot to wash it off!' she cried as she ran into the bathroom." It's a facial health pack!" she yelled. "Mary Ann gave me the beauty recipe from an ancient oriental book. It's made of mushrooms and oils mixed with avocado and beaten eggs.

It is a preservative!'"

"Does it preserve you after death or before?" I asked.

"What did you say?" she called to me. A few minutes later Jody came into the bedroom looking and smelling her beautiful, normal self again,

"I'm sorry, Michael."

"Bet you were just getting even with me for the fish episode the other morning." I said with a laugh as I kissed her.

"Tomorrow, liebchen, I'll buy you all the perfumed facial mixtures you could possibly want. But believe me, you don't need them. I love your face exactly the way it is, and I will from day to day, year to year as we grow old together for the next hundred years. Nothing will ever change that. Now, let's air out the room!"

Our honeymoon days at the lake came to an end. As we walked to the little boat to take us to the mainland Jody threw a kiss in the air and said,

"I loved every minute with you, little island. Michael, you know during these two weeks it's been as if we were in our own remote paradise on earth, our own Shangri-1a." At that moment I was tempted to call the owner and see if we could rent the place for the rest of the summer but I remembered he had told me these were the only two weeks it was available and besides, Jody was looking forward to traveling up through Canada.

We got into the little boat with our suitcases and went across the lake to where our car was left and returned the keys from the house and boat to the attendant.

Jody's eyes were sparkling. The sun from the past few days had streaked her hair with gold. She looked as if she had stepped out of a Titian painting.

"Civilization", she smiled and squeezed my hand tightly and lovingly.

TWENTY

The Untold Story

As we made our way north we came into a small, quaint sea town where Jody noticed a gift shop next to a gas station. While I filled the tank with gas Jody filled her arms with presents to bring home to our friends. Down the street we came to a restaurant that advertised 'Home-made Fish Chowder and Seafood'. It was already lunch time and the aroma coming from the restaurant was hard to pass by so we pulled in and enjoyed a filling and exceptionally good lunch. We were about to order the apple pan dowdy dessert that looked so good at the next table when a newsboy came into the place yelling in a high pitched voice, "Extra! Extra! Read all about it! Hitler, Killer of Millions is Alive! The Fuhrer has been found!" Jody and I looked at each other. A pitch of excitement filled the restaurant. Everyone was talking at once.

"Well I'll be!" Jody exclaimed, I always suspected that monster had escaped !"

"It's not too hard to conceive once you think about it Jody. Martin Bormann escaped and Mengele escaped. So if these murderers, and so many more who were low men on the totem pole got away, why not Hitler ? Most generals and their advisors always planned in advance how they would escape in case they didn't win the wars they started. And with all the money, the loot and treasures which that murderer Hitler took from the people he had killed, he could have easily paid his way into any country where he had supporters! Besides, they never found his body, only teeth, and those could have been a fake."

I called the newsboy over to our table and bought a paper. My eyes glued to the picture on the front page, my head began to throb and I became numb. Jody, on seeing my face took the paper from my hand. "Oh no, this can't be!" She quickly put her cold hand on mine. Her voice trembled with disbelief as she stared at the picture.

A large, elderly woman sitting next to us started to cry, "My boy was killed at Dunkirk, and that fiend is still alive!"

Her voice echoed in my ears, over and over I heard in my head, "that fiend, that fiend.' I felt sick, completely disoriented and unable to say a word. I had broken into a sweat. I heard Jody cry out,

"Michael, it can't be! This is a horrible, horrible mistake! This couldn't possibly be him! It just couldn't be!" she cried. I looked at her not really seeing anything but felt her tugging at my arm.

"Michael, people are looking at us. Let's leave." I wiped my forehead on the sleeve of my shirt, automatically paid the check and quickly walked away from the curious staring eyes.

"Come on Jody, we'll call my folks." I said as I ran to the nearest pay phone and dialed the number. A fear crept into me when the operator announced in a machine like manner, "The telephone number you have just called has been changed to an unpublished number." I hollered, "Operator, I've got to reach them! It's my family. I've got to have their number!"

"I am sorry but we are not at liberty to give out this information." I hung up, unable to think of what to do next.

"Call your Uncle at his office, Michael!" I got information and put in the call to Ludwig, but they told me he wasn't there. Angrily, I banged down the phone. After talking a few minutes we decided to take the car to the airport, fly to Washington and see my parents. Jody kept trying to reassure me and probably herself at the same time that this was all a mistake but I became more nervous as I sat in the plane and read the newspapers which exposed my Grandfather's face to the world. They described him as 'The Devil, The Killer of Millions, and the Mastermind of Death'. The articles said he had accidentally been found among a group of men the F.B.I. had been watching for some time. They had arrested this group in connection with a plot to assassinating public figures and in connection with the bombing of public buildings. The F.B.I. named them as part of a Nazi group which has been growing here in the United States, South America, abroad and especially in Germany.

Another newspaper said that in 1976 alone, forty-one thousand young men in Germany had avoided the eighteen month draft into the government's federal republic army called the Bundeswehr, and instead were becoming part of a New Nazi Era, which showed a reverence for Hitler and anti-Semitism. Hitler's arrest capped a two year investigation in which undercover F.B.I. agents infiltrated the Nazi group. Still another article said the Kennedy assassination, President Reagan's assault, and the kidnappings of big industrialist, all over the world had been linked to the Nazis.

It said the United States Government was keeping Adolf Hitler hidden from the public until psychiatric testing and questioning could take place and that it was very questionable as to what would be done with him.

Each special edition came out with thoughts on what might be done with this leader of a sinister force that still overshadowed the earth. Would he become just another unpunished war criminal because of his age? Would he spend the rest of his days in a 'so-called' jail? Would he be put in a rest home for the mentally insane for which the taxpayers would pay? Some wondered if he would be sent back to Germany, and end up helping with the New Nazi Movement!

I tried to light up my pipe but my hand shook, and I was unable to control it.

Deep down a terrified feeling came over me as a sudden picture of my Grandfather's personality flashed into my mind and it paralleled many things I had read about Hitler. Jody looked searchingly at me.

"The history books all say he killed himself. Maybe your Grandfather confessed to being Hitler because he had delusions. Many people his age get hardening of the arteries in the head and think they are other people. He couldn't be." She stopped. She couldn't even say the name, as if mentioning it would make it become a reality.

I looked at her, and then tried to continue to read. The many incidents that happened during the past years started flooding my mind. The way my Father and Mother always seemed to watch Grandfather, quieting him when he started to talk too much. At the time, I thought they were concerned with his health, but he was a strong old man who looked and acted much younger than his years. I started remembering the things I had read about Hitler, his boyhood, his education, his painting. Grandfather had even discussed Hitler with me! I remembered how upset Mother would get whenever he would go to one of his meetings. How upset Grandfather looked when he found out Jody was Jewish. But my Father, his son-in-law, has been working for the

United States Government in the Immigration Department for years! He was the head of it. Grandfather was even called for jury duty! It didn't make sense, but if it were true look what I did to Jody! The thoughts wouldn't stop. Hitler was suppose to be a vegetarian and wouldn't smoke or drink, neither did my Grandfather, neither did a lot of people I tried to tell myself. I broke into a cold sweat and a wave of nausea hit me.

"Michael, you're not listening to me."

"I'm sorry Jody. What did you say?" "I said, I'm afraid to call my folks. They may have seen the newspapers and possibly connected some of the names."

"Maybe you should go home to them till this blows over, one way or another."

"This horrible thing can't be true, Michael!"

"We said ourselves Jody, other important men in the Nazi party got away." She looked at me without any words. What was left to say?

After the plane landed in Washington we grabbed a cab to take us to Sonnenblume. As we got out of the taxi someone appeared from nowhere and tried to photograph us. I quickly raised my arm to shield Jody's face and mine and as the camera flashed we ran up the marble stairs and rang the bell. As we waited I noticed two men standing nearby who seemed to be watching the house. From behind the bushes two boys ran out and yelled,

"Nazi lovers!" I immediately took out my old house key from my pocket and unlocked the front door. As we walked in the sound of sobbing came from the living room. My Mother was sitting on the couch crying, her face red and eyes swollen, beside her was my Father. As soon as she saw me she burst out "Michael!" and ran to me.

She wrapped her arms tightly around me and cried and shook like I had never seen before.

It was then I knew what I feared was true! I pushed her away gently, as Jody's eyes met mine.

"What is all this about?" I asked angrily.

"It's been terrible, Michael. Mother answered, "The reporters have been hounding us day and night. We were getting so many obscene phone calls we had to change our number. And the mail we don't dare read it when it comes here! Your Father has been temporarily dismissed until further investigation. Believe me Michael, your Father never did anything wrong! Now the question is what the United States Government will do with us".

"Are you two involved with what's going on?"

"Oh, no!" Mother continued hysterically, "but they are making a big fuss out of everything they can! Just because my Father was the leader of a Nazi Group!" she cried. "After all these years it's ridiculous! He is an old man and there were many people like him that encouraged and helped him and they are not being persecuted! They rose to high positions everywhere after the war. This government is causing Grandfather such grief that his blood pressure will surely go up. He could have a stroke!!"

She lay down on the couch and Father put a wet compress on her head that Helga, the housekeeper, brought in.

"Do you realize what you're telling us?" I asked.

"You're saying this man, your Father, the man I called Grandfather all my life is Hitler! And you're only worried he will get a stroke? My own flesh and blood is a mass murderer, a real living, Satan!" I yelled as I paced up and down the long living room. He and the cesspool of humanity who joined him tortured and destroyed millions of people in their concentration camps. He caused the worst catastrophe of bloodshed in the history of the world! Not only against Jews, but non Jews, too! Don't you want to realize who your Father is?" "Michael," my Mother abruptly interrupted, "certainly all the people from all over the world, who contributed to the Nazi cause like wealthy socialites, the nobility, industrialists, bankers, political scientists were not, as you put it, 'the cesspool of humanity.' Your Grandfather has been entertained and accepted by the cream of world society, even to today! My Father never told a lie, Michael. His book, Mein Kampf, was read by many, many people and was pregnant with his ideas about regenerating the world. The world's most powerful people undermined the Social Democrats in Germany and supported your Grandfather with the hope that Russia and the Jews would

be wiped out!'"

"Do not say he is my Grandfather! My Grandfather is now dead to me! Hitler should never have had a grandchild." I shouted as my Father said, "Tell him!'"

"Tell me what?" I asked, as a strange look passed between my parents. My Mother cried, "Your Father wants me to tell you how we all loved you and how we still love you and that all this has nothing to do with you. We tried to keep you out of it. That's why we never told you anything."

"That is not what I wanted you to tell him! He has a right to know! My Father said.

A long deep silence fell over the room. "Your Father just wants me to tell you that you and Jody should move away before you get pulled into this mess."

Jody, who sat with tears in her eyes said with an unsteady quiver in her voice

"To think that my family, my grandparents, children, babies and loved ones in every country perished in the holocaust and today we sit here and have to listen to a defense of Hitler!" She sobbed into her handkerchief as I tried to take her hand but she fled from the room. I followed her and knocked on the bathroom door.

"Jody," I called. "Leave me alone, Michael. Please, let me alone,"

Just then Helga ran to the front door, opened it and screamed in her broken English, "Svines! Svines! Cars, the grounds they are surrounded by cars. Every vun is looking. Home they should go and mind their business! Ve are not freaks to be stared at!"

I banged my hand against the side of my forehead.

"I can't believe it! Hitler is my Grandfather? Everyone thought he was dead! They even said they found his teeth."

"That was planned years before he disappeared from Germany." Father said, "The truth is that he and his wife Eva, were secretly married for years." "Yes," my Mother continued, "they had me raised quietly away from everyone under another name. But in April 1945 they realized that the allies were advancing into Berlin and that it was imminent that the Russians were going to take the city, so we prepared to leave Berghof, Eagles Nest. I remember it to every detail. We were picked up by a four engine Heinkel plane

that could easily take off from our mountain region.

It was piloted by my Father's favorite pilot, Hans Rudel, who we now call Kemka. We flew to Asia, and that night Berlin surrendered to the Allies. Then when it was safe we flew to South America and then the United States. We moved around quite a bit, to be sure we were safe. My Father had many German connections in this country and had brought a great deal of money and jewels with him. But it was shortly after coming here that my Mother died. She died in her sleep. She was beautiful and a wonderful Mother. I will never forget her." she said as she wiped her eyes. "Eventually I went to college and met your Father, who had also escaped from Germany, and was studying law. He started working in a law firm in New York and it wasn't long before your Father and I fell in love and decided to marry and move to New Jersey."

Mother wiped her eyes again as she reflected back, "Shortly afterwards your Father started working for the government's immigration department and in a few years you were a part of our lives. That is when we made our final move here to Sonnenblume, and Grandfather moved in with us. We were always very happy here. We had everything we wanted."

"I am sure you did have everything you wanted which was paid for by the blood of millions!" I said with contempt.

'Your Grandfather was an extreme genius of a man. You have to try to understand," my Mother said. "He was hated because he had a dream. It was a dream of a Master Race!" I sat there and laughed, "Is that why you think he is hated, because of a dream?

"Michael, Mother said, we who lived with him and knew him well saw the gentleness in him. He adored animals, especially dogs. I remember one day when his canary died," she sniffed, "and he actually cried. You know he would never eat meat because he felt it was barbaric to hunt animals! Michael, don't laugh. I know what you are thinking, but he was an unusual genius."

"He was a madman! A psychopath! Why don't you see it?" I yelled at her. "But Michael, I'm talking about the part of him which I knew. He was a

wonderful Father, he loved all children."

"Even the ones he had destroyed or mutilated?" I looked at this women who was my Mother and realized she was someone I never really knew,

"Mother," I said, "your Father ordered his Nazi soldiers to take infants by their ankles and smash their heads against brick buildings in front of their Mothers, and you have the nerve to tell me he cried over a canary!" I felt myself laughing, laughing quite uncontrollably.

"Michael, stop upsetting your Mother. Just remember Hitler was wonderful to my parents in Germany, my sister and my brother Ludwig."

Father said

"Ludwig, knew who he was?"

"Of course he knew everything. In time you will get over the shock."

"I will never forget or forgive any of you! Look how well you covered up for him! I didn't even suspect who he was. You should have told me!' Now I've involved a wife in this mess! A wife whose own family suffered from him! Had I known I would never have married!"

"Stop it Michael!" My Father shouted. "Your Mother is in a state of collapse as it is. The doctor left just before you came in." He called Helga to bring my Mother her medicine.

"What happened wasn't my Father's fault." My Mother persisted. "He was told terrible things about the Jews in his childhood days at school in Austria, which he believed. I also learned that as Father grew up he read books and magazines which were filled with anti-Semitism. Grandfather even felt a Jewish doctor killed his Mother!"

"But every book says his Mother died of cancer!" I shouted, "No doctor could have cured her. She died like thousands of people are still dying from it today."

"My Father also told me that the Jews on the Art Academy's Board kept him from getting into their school when he was a young boy." She said

"You're telling me these are the reasons that he persecuted and killed so many millions of Jews? What kind of a woman are you? I used to think you were an intelligent person. Tell me, since he was your Father, why didn't you object to my marrying a Jew?"

"It was for safety reasons that I didn't object, your safety Michael. You're being married to a Jewess meant less chance of discovery. It was for you, our child's protection."

"You mean for your Nazi Fathers protection!"

"Michael, we love you." she said. "You are our only child. It was a long time before we even had you. I didn't think I would ever have a child. Don't blame us too much."

Jody came into the living room, her face contorted and her eyes swollen. My Mother looked at her. "I realize this is a terrible shock to you, being Jewish and all. I'm sure you feel we did you an injustice.

"You could never understand how torn-apart I am! You people could not possibly understand the human feelings of those who have suffered. When have you ever suffered?

Now I am just afraid of the pain my parents may yet feel, the pain that I contribute to their lives. I only hope and pray they never find out about this horrible family relationship! It would kill them! Jody sobbed.

I noticed my Father whisper to my Mother as her eyes flashed him an angry look before she said again,

"If you move away you may not get involved. Don't stay around this part of the country. Anything can happen if you do. It is very dangerous! Things can start coming out about you and who you are, where you work and where you live. People will go looking for you. People look for retaliation. Your lives will be threatened by people who want to get back at us through you. We are moving in with friends next week. It isn't safe for us here. Did you see the plain clothes men watching the house as you came in? This is what it will be like for you if they find out who you are. People were throwing rocks at our home before. You two will be targets not only for rocks but for every money making scheme. People will want to read about you. You won't have a private life. Obscenity will be spewed on you!'

"I don't like running away." I said.

"Your dedication now is to your wife, Michael." Mother continued, "What do you think people will do with a Jewish girl who married Hitler's grandson?"

"But I didn't know and Michael didn't know! It's not our fault!" Jody screamed.

"That does not matter, my Mother said. They will ridicule you. They will ostracize you. You will not be physically safe! And as you said, Judith, you will make your own family unhappy if you stay around here and they find out. Your family will be harassed by their own people because of you and Michael, being who you are."

"She is right you should listen to her!" Father said

Jody walked back and forth twisting her handkerchief with both hands," I don't know. I don't know what to do. I have to think." she said, almost to herself.

We called a cab and were about to leave when Mother came over to me with open arms, "Mein lieber, lieber sohn", she cried. (my dearest, dearest son) "Don't Mother". I said as I lifted my hands to prevent her embrace. She turned and covered her face with her hands and cried out to me, "Don't blame me for who my Father is, Michael."

"I'm not blaming you Mother. That is not your fault, but you should have told me! I can't forgive you for that!"

My Father and I looked at each other, knowing without words we may never see each other again.

Jody and I flew back to Maine, picked up our car, and drove on to Boston. "I will never be able to face people who suffered from the Nazis, like

Grandma Kravitz, or your family, Jody."

"We may never have to face my family, Michael." I looked at her anxiously as we drove homeward. After awhile, she said unconvincingly, "We can't torture ourselves over happenings that we had nothing to do with Michael. In a way, the people we are born to are just an accident of nature over which we have no control. What is killing to realize," she continued, angrily, "is that he caused such a painful sorrowful upheaval to the whole world and went on to live such a wonderful life!"

Jody and I went about our daily existence. The happiness, the effervescence seemed to have drained out of our marriage. I tried to write. Each day I sat at the typewriter and stared at the sheet of blank paper. Because of Hitler being found every newspaper I picked up had stories about the Nazi Era of the thirties. But they completely ignored the Nazi problem of today. It seemed so ironic in view of the fact that the same Nazism that was evident then is today in the United States, Germany, Great Britain, South America and all over the world. That must have been why my Grandfather traveled so much, I thought to myself, especially to South America. It was there that Dr. Josef Mengele, 'the Angel of Death' and Dr. Walter Schreiber, who practiced his gruesome experiments on Nazi prisoners were hiding.

Mengele's was the medical scientist who practiced on prisoners in the concentration camps how to turn brown eyes to blue without use of painkillers. Schreiber practiced his medical science on women prisoners by cutting their legs and putting ground glass and wood shavings into their open wounds. Paraguay continued to extend the Holocaust by giving them a sanctuary,

I said to myself.

As the summer ended I decided to send in my resignation to the school. Judith insisted,

"Michael, don't make a hasty decision. We're still emotionally distraught." "I have no intention of teaching ancient history anymore and besides under the circumstances I cannot face all those people in the school, even if

they don't know who I really am. I know who I am!"

"How do you think I feel?" she asked. "I hate myself too. I hate what may become of you because of what you come from!"

We stared at each other. Her feelings were now out in the open. I turned away from her, ashamed, only to look into the mirror, another reminder of where I come from.

The phone calls came in from friends who thought I quit teaching to write another book. I didn't want to see or talk to anyone. Each day after school Judith would come in and cheerfully start talking.

"Everyone misses you at school." and then go into her psychological bit on, 'togetherness.'

"Michael, we will get through this thing together. We can go away together."

I started feeling resentful of everything, even Judith. I couldn't stop myself. There were moments I felt like yelling at her and many times I   did. I told her and myself she would be better off leaving me and I thought perhaps she would. Many nights I couldn't fall asleep until four or five in the morning and then I would sleep for the whole day. Some days Judith would wake me for supper, but most of the time she ate alone. It was the middle of September when the mailman brought me a small check from the publisher of my history book.

"Michael, we have got to do something to earn more money. I won't be working after this month."

"Quit your job if you want." I told her. "I don't want to quit. I have to leave." "You have to leave?"

"They won't let a teacher work after her third month." "Did you say, third month?"

"I am pregnant! It happened on the island." I was thunderstruck! "Are you sure?"

"I went to Cynthia's obstetrician last week. He's positive. Now we will have to think of someone else besides ourselves. As far as money, you can always write some magazine articles or maybe another book or maybe a novel and"

"I do not want a baby!"

"Michael, stop it! I'm not any happier about it now than you are! But I'm in my third month. I hoped you might at least be nice about it. I thought this might help straighten out our problems.

"I don't want any kid, now or ever!"

"You don't mean that Michael. You don't really mean" "Get rid of it! Go to a doctor."

"You want me to destroy our child?"

"He wouldn't be just ours Jody. He would be a remnant from my past! I would look at him and wonder who he would take after, would he be like 'Him'?"

"But you're not like 'Him'. At least you weren't when I married you. You were a wonderful human being."

"But when I look in the mirror I don't see a wonderful human being. I don't even see a man anymore Jody! I see Hitler's grandson staring back at me and I am afraid! I I am afraid maybe there is something in me that is like 'Him', that has not yet showed itself." I turned away feeling the tears smarting my eyes as Jody rushed over and hugged me to her body.

"Michael, Michael, you're not like 'Him!" What do I have to say to convince you? And our child would not have to find out about 'Him!'"

"My Mother didn't think I would find out either and look what happened! I don't want anymore suffering caused by my ancestor! I don't want my child to inherit a birthright of shame!" As I pride myself loose from her arms I said, "I don't want any children Judith, not now or ever! If you don't want to live with me under these conditions, it's up to you."

"I understand how you must feel but I could never do away with our child. I would never be able to live with myself!"

"Jody, I'm very serious about this. Nobody can understand how I feel, nobody! Not even you. You want me to feel that 'His' life has nothing to do with mine but it does! My family's guilt is my guilt! Your people were victims, and that is sad. Mine are criminals and that is shameful. I don't want to discuss it again." I went into my room, back to bed exhausted. The next morning Judith told me that I had tossed and turned so much in my sleep that I whacked her in the stomach. From then on she slept alone on the couch. The times she tried to reach me, to touch me, I turned away. All physical desire was dead within me. All I wanted was to be left alone.

"Michael, why are you torturing yourself and me?" she would cry. "We can't help what happened before we were born and we can't help that we fell in love! Believe me, I feel plenty of guilt. It's not easy for me!"

Jody kept trying to get me to go for professional help. "Cynthia's uncle is a psychologist and they say he's very good and"

"And you've been discussing me with everyone?" I yelled. "There is nothing wrong with me that a psychologist can help! You can help me. Just get off my back!"

She looked at me stunned. I turned and went into 'my' bedroom, for that is what it had become. I closed the door and took out a bottle of scotch I had hidden under the bed.

As time went by I found I was fighting a mental war within myself, tortured by thoughts of killings and deaths. The things I had read about Hitler kept pushing their way into my mind. How he had murdered the German Socialists, murdered the German Democrats, murdered the German Resistance and the German Communists. And in his demand for blind obedience and devotion the fiend even hacked to death members of his own Nazi Party like Ernst Roehm. Any one who did not agree wit him he got rid of!

I could not accept the fact that my family was responsible for these crimes! The greatest robber in the world and the greatest mass murderer was my own flesh and blood! I could not live with myself. I had no self respect left.

Charles tried several times to get me on the phone but I did not feel like listening to him so I pretended to be asleep or resting when Judith told me that he was calling. He finally gave her the message that he would be over to see me the next day.

Just before his expected visit I detoured my way to the Horseshoe Tavern and slipped into the farthest booth at the rear of the room. Hopefully, I would escape Charles and my thoughts for a few hours with a bottle of scotch. When I came home Judith simply told me that Grandma Kravitz had invited us for dinner, not mentioning that Charles had been there.

"You go. I have already had my dinner." I said feeling miserable. Jody's voice rose,

"You are being miserable to all your friends, Michael!"

"If they knew who I was they wouldn't want me for their friend or you either!" I yelled back.

She slammed the door shut and left. Meanwhile I finished the rest of my bottle and fell asleep at the kitchen table until she returned and said,

"Michael, it's time to go to bed." Her voice sounded like a distant echo and my head felt as if someone had dropped a lead pipe on it. My body was hot but I shivered with the chills, and my mouth tasted as if I had just eaten burnt ashes. Judith came over and put her hand sympathetically on mine, but I pushed it aside and ran to the bathroom to vomit. When I regained myself I shuffled back to the kitchen.

"Michael, this is no way to solve a problem." she said as she picked up the empty bottle of scotch and looked at it.

"Don't get on my back and don't lecture! Just make me some black coffee." I told her as I put my head in my hands to keep the kitchen light from stabbing at my eyes.

The months began to slip by but things didn't get any better. It became an effort for me to even shave. I lifted the razor, dropped it and went back to the bedroom and flopped into the lounge chair to smoke my pipe. Judith and I communicated less and less. Whenever we spoke it ended in an argument. I sometimes thought if it weren't for her being pregnant that she would have left me. I certainly was not a pleasure to be around.

But as the cold winter months progressed she started to spend all her free time at home painting pictures, which she sent to New York to be sold through her old friend, Bernie Goldberg. She would hum and sing as she worked on her latest canvas of a little boy at the seashore. It seemed to keep her happy while she was waiting for the baby.

This particular night I was in a very irritable mood and her humming annoyed me to such an extent that I grabbed a brush, and splashed paint all over the child's face. Without a word she seized her coat and was about to run out of the apartment when I pulled her to me and put my face against her breast as I cried,

"I am so sorry I dragged you into this. I feel so guilty that I made you a part of this horrible life of mine, Jody, Jody, will you ever be able to forgive me for what I did to you!"

She lifted my face between her hands and we looked into each other's eyes for the first time in months as she said,

"Michael, I don't believe children should suffer for the sins of their fathers. I love you. I want to help you and I need you to help me. Please Michael, let us help each other."

It was later the next day that Jody called me to the telephone. "Your Mother wants to speak to you Michael."

"Tell her I can't talk."

"Michael, she insists it's very important. Unwillingly, I walked to the phone. Mother cried in my ear.

"Your Grandfather will be going on trial. They are trying to decide when and where it will be. I wanted to tell you before you read it in the newspapers."

Resentfully I said, "I'm sure he will get the best treatment with his 'pay off 'money, he always has!"

"Please don't be so callous Michael. Let us try and make all this up to you. We have more money than we know what to do with, let us send you some. "Don't shame me any further, Mother. I wouldn't take his blood money." "Michael, your Grandfather was good to you when you were growing up.

He taught you everything he knew."

"I'm learning by myself now Mother, the one thing he knew best and never taught me."

"What was that Michael?" "How to hate!"

TWENTY ONE

The Trial

Sleep became a fear, as each nightmare became more horrible than the last. I walked the floors until the early hours of the morning, waiting for exhaustion to overcome me. Many a night I would awaken dazed as to where I was. Jody shook me, trying to make me coherent. Michael, wake up! Wake up!" she repeated, "You were moaning and yelling in your sleep."

I stared at her blinking, not knowing who she was. She would wipe my wet forehead and change my pajamas that were drenched and dripping with perspiration. The dreams were always the same about the horrible cruelties of the concentration camps, the persecution, the torture and the slaughter of unarmed mothers, fathers, sisters, brothers, babies and the elderly, the refuse of crippled and wounded young men, the horrible experiments on Christians and Jews that the Nazi doctors performed.

Now the newspapers were filled with plans for Hitler's trial. I became physically ill and Jody insisted on calling a doctor who gave me medication. I slept around the clock and dreamed about a huge outdoor coliseum filled with thousands of people from all corners of the globe.

Suddenly, a thunderous voice cried out to me,

"This is the trial of Adolph Hitler against humanity! It was Adolf Hitler who premeditated a program of genocide unequalled in history against the defenseless and peaceful Jewish people. Adolf Hitler is accused of giving the orders for the "final solution." He alone, the head of a regime who practiced scientific savagery against Belgians, Danes, Russians, Poles, Germans,

Communists, Socialists, French, Dutch, Norwegians, and thousands more."

There he sat in the center of the coliseum as dark clouds drifted over the ghostly faces of the people who had suffered and died from this evil creature.

"The blame is not mine alone! I did not invent Nazism." The creature cries out. "I did not invent anti-Semitism, evil or cruelty, persecution, intolerance, concentration camps, passion plays, funeral pyres or massacres. I was influenced by centuries of hate! Concentration camps go back to the ancient pagan vorld and ver used by empire builders centuries ago! Hate flourished before me! Hate flourished during the Inquisition, the Holy Crusades, the killings of the Huguenots, the Albigensians, the Thirty Year Var, the forced conversion of the American Indian and all the Vars in Europe!"

I heard his voice scream with tense emotion as he stated,

"I vas only the Drummer for the Nazi Party. It all started before me. All over Germany after Vorld Var Vun and before, there ver secret societies like the Free Corps, the Vril, the Thule and others. One had to be pure blooded German to belong! They ver all Nationalistic, anti the Veimar Republic, the Constitution, Democracy and all were anti-Semetic! They felt that they should be made into one party."

I kept hearing him plead his case.

"They had their brother fraternities, in America it vas called the Nazi Bund, and in England it vas called the Golden Dawn. Dietrich Eckart, the writer and journalist, vas the Father of Nazi thought, not me! Alfred Rosenberg, the architect who escaped the Russian Revolution vas the philosopher of the movement. Not me! Guttfried Feder vas a renowned professor of political science and he founded the Nazi Party, not me! I vas asked to join the Nazi party. I became the political protigê of Dietrich Eckart because every vun saw that ven I spoke I vas able to convey the passion that we all felt about uniting the vorld and getting rid of evil! Anti-Semitism vas alvays an effective tool and since it vas international it vas necessary to use it vunce again to help our Nazis rise to power. Ve ver able to get money from Jew haters all over the vorld! They caused the var, by giving us money, that vas our ammunition.

Vithout their hate there vould haf been no var! It vas their fault, not mine! Do not think that I am so stupid as to really believe in the superiority of pure blood! I knew it vas a lie about race superiority and blonde, blue eyed Aryans. I knew there ver light, vite, blue eyed Jews depending on vhere their ancestors ver from!

I saw him stand and gesture fiercely with his hands and try to hypnotize the masses as he had in years gone by.

"There ver brilliant scientists, not me, who believed that through a controlled Darwinism ve could create supermen and vomen. They vould be trained in special schools to rule the masses and vould unite the vorld into von Reich vit von Fuhrer to lead them. They vanted me, I should lead them! Killing Jews vas part of a game vunce again, and in 1935 people came from all over the vorld to attend the Passion Plays and before they left they gave us huge sums of money. I didn't ask for it. I didn't vant it!

But vot I did do vas unite Germany! I made Germany rich! I gave everyone a job! Never before did so many people have jobs!'

An old man cried out and three crippled men hobbled towards Hitler. "We know the jobs you gave them! In the concentration camps the scientists and gas men supervised suffocation the people. The electricians were employed hooking electric wires to genital organs. The butchers and surgeons were busy dismembering people so they could make lampshades from the skins. The barbers were employed making pillows from the human hair. The cosmeticians were busy changing human fat into soap. All were occupied with breeding German, blond, blue eyed Aryans to become Fuhrers of the Future!"

"Ve vanted young, healthy men to rule the vorld! Hitler yelled

"You had young, healthy men like me killed!" cried a voice from the crowd.

Hitler denied everything.

"It never happened!" he shouted, throwing his hands in the air. The voices in my nightmare went on,

"When Albrecht Haushofer and his White Rose Resistance Group gathered up against their own Nazi fathers, you had these young men beheaded!"

Hitler did not choose to hear and continued in my mind.

"Everyone approved of vat I vas doing and supported me! Goebbels, believed in me. Anti-Semites, and all those against Russia and communism and the social democratic system supported me. Speer directed my armament industry. There ver Nazis in every country of the vorld who vanted to help me. There had been persecution and burning of the Jews at the stake for fifteen hundred years. I did nothing new! Vot did I do any different from anyvon else? Besides, I vas only following the guidance of Providence and the stars in remaking the vorld, and to do this other people had to suffer, besides the Jews. People from all parts of the vorld ver punished ven they interfered vith my Master Plan! That vas not my fault! In every var in history innocent people haff been killed! Before the ink vas dry on the Treaty of Versailles, the arms manufacturers all over the vorld sold their weapons to German buyers so ve could build Germany up as a bulwark against communism, so they too must also share in vot I did!"

As he went on I saw dark clouds pass over the sick faces and torn crippled bodies of the thousands of people in the huge outdoor coliseum. The angry people moved restlessly. One group after another dragged themselves down the stairs towards their evil enemy. There were many with one leg on crutches, some in wheelchairs, others had fingers missing from their hands, most had scar marked faces. Their bodies moved as if racked with pain and some dripped with blood.

"We are Dutch, not Jews." one grotesque group cried out. "Your SS men beat us every day with iron pipes in your concentration camps! Look what you made of us, you fiend!"

Others in my nightmare screamed,

"Our bodies were thrown into wheelbarrows with the other dead Norwegians, French, Germans, Russians and Poles. We were taken to the building with the tall chimney and our bodies went up in smoke! You are

Satan!" Still they walked, they hobbled, they dragged themselves down from those high stairs in the huge coliseum to face the monster of cruelty, as the dark clouds hovered over head.

"We were Belgians, Yugoslavians, Bulgarians, Hungarians, not Jews. Look what you did to us! Look at our hands, our broken fingers, our dead flesh! You made us dig the graves for our own people, our own families with our bare hands, day, after day, after day! "

With lowered heads and slumped bodies the group shuffled past Hitler and another group dragged their painful bodies towards him, each helping the other, the blind leading the blind.

"We were your own German soldiers. You took our eyes away on the battlefield! You sent us, your young German boys to suffer! The world forgets that you took more than six million Jews to the gas chambers. The world forgets about the five million others that paid with their lives. They forget about the prisoners of war, Jehovah's Witnesses,

priests, nuns, political prisoners and non Jewish resisters who all went to the gas chambers and up the chimney! This was all because you wanted to take over the world!"

Hitler sat with a frozen look on his face as if he expected to be attacked physically at any moment. He did not say a word.

Old, ugly women looked at him and cried,

"We were not Jews. We were Finns. We were British. We were Rumanians. We were beautiful! You made us work in your ammunition plants by day and all your brutal soldiers raped us night after night!"

Other women screeched,

"He dehumanized us! We were his German people and we had to watch our young sons become sadistic men who poured scalding water over old women's heads!"

As the dark clouds moved others cried,

"We are the dead British humanists. You punished us in Treblinka. You had us thrown into open graves and while we were still alive you covered us with earth!"

I heard voices ablaze with anger,

"'We will never forget the days or the moments when your Nazi henchmen came to our homes and dragged our fathers, mothers, and children from their beds. Some of us were restrained and made to watch while your men took their axes and beheaded our families! Our families were good people, kind people. We still see them, their heads severed from their bodies. We still hear your soldier laughing."

"We are Russian men, not Jewish, We came back from the grave to see you punished. You had our young beautiful wives starved and beaten with whips when someone tried to escape from your concentration camp. You had their long beautiful hair pulled out by its roots and you made us watch them die, barbarian, demon, savage!" they yelled as they spit on Hitler and pushed themselves away in their wheelchairs.

Shrill voices screamed out as they moved around Hitler,

"We did not want to die by the hands of your SS murderers but we did not want to stay alive to see our handsome sons bodies dragged out and chopped up to pieces!" The women sobbed. "Your murderers said they were looking for the diamonds and wealth that we may have tried to hide in our bodies!"

Suddenly, Hitler let loose.

"What happened vas not my fault! I could not help the killings of other people. It is alvays vot happens ven der is a var, always through history! I thought if I got rid of the Jews I vould become a savior in the eyes of the vorld! But I vill not be punished!"

He screamed like a wildman. "I haff my friends in the highest places in the governments. My Elite Corp., my SS Men, all over the vorld! They vill not let me be punished! My old age vill protect me! Nazism vill live! Ve may haff lost the var but even now, again today in America, I am praised, respected and loved by thousands of Nazis, who still say, 'Today Germany! Tomorrow the vorld! Deutschland uber alles! (Germany above all) My friends know that democracy and liberty are enemies of our type of dictatorship! These things are against my ideals!

Today another Nazi generation is being rallied together and it's called, The Fourth Reich!' People have already forgotten the millions of Christians that ver killed. But my people vill remember me as a great leader! They haff forgotten the other things. That is why even now, our great German scientists are vorking on the next German army made up completely of clones, in my image! They vill take over the vorld!"

Again I started hearing the voices.

"How can we forget the people beaten with iron rods who were too sick to work,

the attack dogs sent out to rip women, men, babies and the elderly apart, the showers where people were told that they would be cleansed but were sprayed with deathly gas instead, the smoke from the ovens where the bodies were cremated? How can we forget that we were punished for one crime, to have been born! How can we forget that these evil crimes were even more barbaric because they were planned by your men who were professors and professional people?"

The voices cried out, "Can any country forget the efforts and deaths of their people who resisted and the deaths of millions of soldiers and sailors and others in every country of the world who lost their lives because of you? Can we forget how the wonderful Christians in the Resistance in many different countries worked to get Jews out of Germany and were caught, tortured, gassed, hung and shot by your Nazi firing squad? Can we forget that our children and their families were sent to concentration camps, and how the Resistance derailed trains, stole supplies and smuggled them over the border, how they kept death tablets on them to use in case they were caught?

"We cannot forget", cried the voices, "how the Resistance smuggled food to our hideout and smuggled information to other Resistance Groups. How they gave money to guards in prisons so they could get food, letters and their underground newspaper to their artist friends and writers who had been committed for knocking the Third Reich! Can we forget when the White Rose Resistance was caught and you had those young boys beheaded?"

We, the Resistance, found it impossible to believe that our German people, who gave birth to an Albert Schweitzer, could change so quickly and become killers because you became our German leader! We were committed to the ideals of democracy and liberty. We believed that an individual had the right to be able to say what he believed. We did not want to support you and the other Nazis who planned to stifle this natural right. We saw the Nazis were a gang who wanted to overthrow other peoples cultures and become lord and masters over them. Now everyone can see that you, Hitler, prepared the way for today's rise of Russian power. You Hitler started the development of atomic weapons and created the ways and means of mass slaughter. Today's world is the legacy of you, Adolf Hitler!"

"You are evil, evil! They all screamed. "You are worse than Ivan the Terrible, Attila the Hun, Genghis Khan! You are evil! You are guilty! You are evil!" The voices screamed to me, as the dark clouds filled the coliseum and the heads, faces and bodies of the ghosts of the past, filled my head

Suddenly, there was a bright flash of lightning and a loud crash of thunder. A hush fell over the thousands of people in the huge coliseum. Again there was a blinding bolt of lightning and a deafening crash of thunder and Hitler crumbled dead on the floor. The people felt the earth shake as a bright light shined from above and a voice cried out from the heavens,

"I am the Lord Jehovah, the God of Abraham, Isaac, Jacob, Ishmael and Moses. Listen, for I speak to all my children. I speak of destruction. I speak of slaughter. And I speak of extinction. I bring a warning but I speak only once!"

Again the lightning came and the thunder cracked!

"I speak of Sodom and Gomorrah and how the smoke of the country went up as the smoke of a furnace. For thou shall feel the rain of brimstone and fire and call it warfare if thou do not defy the hate in thy wicked hearts for thy brothers of all faiths."

Again the lightning came and the thunder crashed. "Remember thy Bible, thy Ten Commandments, and have no other gods before me!"

150

TWENTY TWO

The Letter

I awoke to see Jody standing over me, her cool, soft hand smoothing my brow. "Michael, are you alright? You've been talking in your sleep and you've been crying out. It almost sounded as if you were praying. You said, 'Bible' and"

"Jody, I had a dream. There was this shining light and I heard a voice." She took my hands in hers and sat down next to me on the bed. "It was as if God was trying to tell me something, Jody. I can't remember it all now but it is very important to me." I started to get out of bed.

"Michael, it was only a dream. Rest so you will feel better. You had a high fever, and you haven't eaten. Let me bring you some food."

"No, I don't need food. It is all clear to me now. There is a purpose for what we have been going through. Our feelings are more than hate for him and his kind. We also have the anger that he has placed on us by this chain of guilt around our necks. The only way to help ourselves is to try and stop his kind of evil, which draws strength from all the evil things around. This need for hate is like that of a vampire who lives off the blood of others. These vampires have caused wars, tried to eliminate an entire Jewish people, killed presidents, individuals, and black children in Atlanta, Georgia. Now they are hungry and waiting for the greatest scientific discovery, nuclear warfare, to gratify their final needs. That is what God tried to warn me about Jody. It is wrong to allow this hate and prejudice of people and nations to cause America to be destroyed like Nineveh and Babylon!

I have a purpose now, and that is to expose these Nazis that still exist and who should be brought to justice and punished. I will write about these murderers who are still alive!

"You can do that with your writing, Michael.

"Even if my Grandfather wasn't who he is, I still would feel the way I do about these barbarians who created such inhuman atrocities, and who still live off the fat of our land! I am going to try and make up for some of the suffering Hitler caused so that you and our baby, and all the other Jody's and babies that come into the world will be free from hate. If I can help make our world a better place to live it will be worth my being born." I cupped her chin in my hand and her eyes looked into mine as I placed my other hand on her stomach. Just then the baby moved. "Jody, I felt our baby! It moved! Our baby moved!"

She laughed. "See, our child wants you to do this for us, Michael." "Yes, now I know everything can be alright as long as we have each other

and hope."

"That is what our child inside me is all about, Michael, hope, a hope for a better tomorrow." As I looked at Jody, I saw her smile suddenly turn to a look of pain.

"Michael, the baby is coming!" She clutched my hand tightly. I held her and then I quickly climbed out of bed, dressed and reached for her coat.

"Come, I'll take you to the hospital, dear." "The pains are going away, Michael."

"We better not wait, Jody." I helped her on with her coat and as we were about to leave someone rang the doorbell. I opened the door and a young man handed me a special delivery letter.

"Come on, Jody. I'll read it later."

"Read it now, Michael, it may be important." We went outside and I tore open the envelope and read it out loud to Jody.

'Dearest Michael,

We know that we have lost you and that you hate us for who we are but please try to remember us for what we tried to be to you.

You are entitled to your self respect, your freedom from guilt. Do not hate yourself anymore for being a part of us. Enclosed you will find your adoption papers.'

Our Love Always, Mother and Dad"

We stared at each other. We hugged. We kissed and tears dripped from Jody's eyes.

"We are so lucky, Michael! Now you, we, our baby, are really free!" She laughed and I laughed and we kissed each other again and again.

"Now you can go and find out who is your real family. Maybe the adoption files are open to the public, Michael."

"No thanks, darling." I said as I held her tightly.

"I already have found my real Father." I looked up at the sun filled sky, smiled and said, "Our Father Who Art In Heaven."

THE END

www.ingramcontent.com/pod-product-compliance
Lightning Source LLC
Chambersburg PA
CBHW040535170726
48295CB00012B/473